STRANGE DOIN'S
IN THE PINE HILLS

Borgo Press Books by Ardath Mayhar

The Absolutely Perfect Horse: A Novel of East Texas (with Marylois Dunn)
The Body in the Swamp: A Washington Shipp Mystery [Wash Shipp #2]
Carrots and Miggle: A Novel of East Texas
The Clarrington Heritage: A Gothic Tale of Terror
Closely Knit in Scarlatt: A Novel of Suspense
Crazy Quilt: The Best Short Stories of Ardath Mayhar
Deadly Memoir: A Novel of Suspense
Death in the Square: A Washington Shipp Mystery [Wash Shipp #1]
The Door in the Hill: A Tale of the Turnipins
The Dropouts: A Tale of Growing Up in East Texas
Feud at Sweetwater Creek: A Novel of the Old West
The Fugitives: A Tale of Prehistoric Times
The Heirs of Three Oaks: A Novel of the Old West
High Mountain Winter: A Novel of the Old West
How the Gods Wove in Kyrannon: Tales of the Triple Moons
Hunters of the Plains: A Novel of Prehistoric America
Island in the Lake: A Novel of Native America
Khi to Freedom: A Science Fiction Novel
The Lintons of Skillet Bend: A Novel of East Texas
Lone Runner: A Novel of the Old West
Lords of the Triple Moons: A Science Fantasy Novel: Tales of the Triple Moons
Makra Choria: A Novel of High Fantasy
Medicine Dream: Being the Further Adventures of Burr Henderson
Messengers in White: A Science Fantasy Novel
Monkey Station: A Novel of the Future (Macaque Cycle #1; with Ron Fortier)
People of the Mesa: A Novel of Native America
A Planet Called Heaven: A Science Fiction Novel
Prescription for Danger: A Novel of the Old West
Reflections; & Journey to an Ending: Collected Poems
A Road of Stars: A Fantasy of Life, Death, Love, and Art
Runes of the Lyre: A Science Fantasy Novel
The Saga of Grittel Sundotha: A Science Fantasy Novel
The Seekers of Shar-Nuhn: Tales of the Triple Moons
Shock Treatment: An Account of Granary's War: A Science Fiction Novel
Slewfoot Sally and the Flying Mule: Tall Tales from Cotton County, Texas
Soul-Singer of Tyrnos: A Fantasy Novel
Strange Doin's in the Pine Hills: Stories of Fantasy and Mystery in East Texas
Strange View from a Skewed Orbit: Autobiographical Reminiscences
Through a Stone Wall: Lessons from Thirty Years of Writing
Timber Pirates: A Novel of East Texas (with Marylois Dunn)
Towers of the Earth: A Novel of Native America
Trail of the Seahawks: A Novel of the Future (Macaque Cycle #2; with R. Fortier)
The Tulpa: A Novel of Fantasy
Two-Moons and the Black Tower: A Novel of Fantasy
Vendetta: A Novel of the Old West
Warlock's Gift: Tales of the Triple Moons
The World Ends in Hickory Hollow: A Novel of the Future
A World of Weirdities: Tales to Shiver By

STRANGE DOIN'S IN THE PINE HILLS

STORIES OF FANTASY AND MYSTERY IN EAST TEXAS

by

Ardath Mayhar

THE BORGO PRESS

An Imprint of Wildside Press LLC

MMIX

CONTENTS

INTRODUCTION

When I was a wee lad, I knew without a doubt that our old, two-story house in Fairview, Massachusetts was filled to the rafters with slinky, slimy monsters. Every morning, I'd creep down the stairs from my second-story bedroom, and very quietly, very stealthily go from window to window in the living room, carefully raising the blinds to let in the light. Otherwise, I knew, it just wasn't safe to play down there, not with everything so dark and creepy and ookey. I mean, kids ken these things instinctively—otherwise, we'd never live past our childhood.

Well, having read the stories in this collection, I now know where all the monsters have gone: *to East Texas*.

Aliens are hiding there, without a doubt (remember *Men in Black*?). So are the leftover remnants of early humanity. The aboriginal Indians—they're there too, lurking in the backwoods, ready to scalp you if you so much as blink an eye sidewise.

That swampy country is full of water moccasins, rattlesnakes, vicious boars (the four-legged kind *and* the two-legged variety), slinky copperheads, open-mouthed gators, snippy little crawfish, giant (need I add, "man-eating") catfish, baby-chasing cougars, B-52-sized skeeters, critters so nasty they don't even have a name, and all sorts of vile sub-species of human lowlife. If they're mean, green, and full of spleen, you'll find 'em lurkin' back in them piney woods, oh yeah.

There's someone else out there too—this li'l ole lady who dwells out in the middle of goddam nowhere in a metal house surrounded by trees. She's survived car crashes and narrow escapes and crashing space shuttles. She's got a loaded .306 stashed in one room, a .45 revolver in another, and a half-dozen others scattered in their hidey-holes—fer shure! You don't want to go messin' around with her—no way, José!

That she also happens to be a great writer is astonishing. And that her overcooked imagination has created all of the creepy-crawlies mentioned above is beyond belief. But it's all true, folks.

I've never actually met Ardath Mayhar in the flesh. I've been assured, though, by the people who know her that she's really a very "nice" person (don't you just love that word!). Hee, hee, hee. You betcha! Very nice! *Bang, bang, you're dead!*

Because that's the way her fiction works, see. You're just rollin' along, enjoying that lovely, leisurely ride through the emerald-hued piney woods of East Texas, and then—*bang, bang, you're dead!* Or some sweet li'l ole nice thing living out in the country lures you into her equally sedate home, offering you a glass of milk and some chocolate chip cookies, and you pop those succulent suckers right down your throat before realizing that she has no whites in her eyes—just little flies—and you're trapped or twisted or tortured or tamed or…whatever evil thing that sweet li'l ole writer lady has dreamed up.

And you never even saw it comin', neither.

I've visited East Texas in these pages, my dear readers, and it's one strange place, let me tell ya. But the damndest thing is—I keep coming back for more! I just can't help myself.

So I put it to ya, gentlebeings one and all: try dipping into this book. Just once! See, I know the outcome of that particular tale.

Betcha can't read just one!

—Robert Reginald
San Bernardino, California
8 June 2009

East Texas abounds with odd people and strange little old ladies. Being one myself, I can vouch for that. And Irene is an example. Also, Wolf was my dog for many satisfactory years, and I still miss him.

THE ARTISTIC TOUCH

The first long cool breath of evening moved the tops of the chinaberry trees shading the yard. Far in the woods beyond the creek an owl began to hoot. It was definitely cooler, Irene decided. Time to take a break from painting.

She moved through the hot, dim house and dropped to sit on the kitchen steps, taking a small sketch pad out of her pocket. That squirrel in the oak, with his tail just so, would work into her next painting. She was sketching busily when the scream brought her head up and sent her sharp gaze toward the creek beyond the fishpond. Was that actually a human scream? Or a screech owl? Or maybe something else?

Irene rose and reached inside the kitchen door for her .410 shotgun. So far out in the country, thirty minutes from the nearest town, she'd taken care of herself for fifty-one years, and she intended to keep right on doing it. No country-bred person could ignore a cry for help, and there was nobody to send to check. By the time she called the sheriff and somebody got there, whatever was going on would be over and done with.

Wolf, three-quarters red wolf, one-quarter German shepherd, came after her as she strode toward the creek. Then, head high, nose at the alert, he moved ahead into the shadows of the sweetgum trees along the stream. He'd scare away any snakes that might be dozing beside the water.

She paused again, listening. That was no screech owl. It sounded like a woman, down there in the thickets along the river. She followed the dog as he lolloped along the cow-path that followed the creek bank. As she drew near the river, Irene took shotgun shells from the string bag that was always tied to the trigger guard of her .410, dropping them into her pocket loose. She always kept one in the chamber.

Two years before, a woman had been killed at the campsite where the road ended at the river. She had no intention of being another. Her mind busy with speculation, she crept on, wondering if some drug deal might have gone wrong at the camp. That had been one of the theories the sheriff mentioned when they found that woman's body.

But it might be a bad child getting his tail swatted too. "Let's not get all melodramatic," she muttered, keeping Wolf's cocked ears in view as he moved through berry vines and button willows to the borrow pit that bordered the road. She cut around the end of that and darted across the rutted mud track into the woods beyond. The camp was not far now, and she didn't want to run into something unexpected.

Again she crept like an Indian, taking care not to crush through deadfall or whip betraying branches. When she came, stooping to stay below the level of the bushes, to the bluff that overlooked the campsite, she lay flat on her belly and stared. A club-cab pickup, its body jacked high on outsized tires, was parked at an angle, almost at the edge of the water. Behind it, a woman lay flat on her face, while a man wielded a stick that came down on her back with cracks like pistol shots.

"Damn whore, hold out on me!"

The words were plain, though they came in grunts between his blows. The woman, evidently too weak now to scream, didn't even flinch. Was she dead? If not, she soon might be.

Irene slid the shotgun forward, pulled back the hammer, and took careful aim. She couldn't kill someone from ambush, she knew, but she could scare the teetotal hell out of him. The gun, small as it was, had a roar like a cannon.

The stick, raised high for another lick at the woman, suddenly became a stub with an end fringed like some giant toothbrush. Stray shot from the pattern evidently struck the man about the face and neck, for he dropped his weapon and began feeling his skin. Then he stopped and stared around him, trying to find the source of the attack.

Irene flattened her face on the ground behind a sugarbush shrub. Wolf lay flat beside her, even his breathing almost silent.

"Damn!" He turned and dived into the pickup. The engine started with a roar; the wheels spun as he backed recklessly to gain turning room. When he gunned it again, the right front wheel ran over the woman's leg, but she gave no sign she had felt it.

Her heart sick with dread, Irene waited until the last sound of the engine died away, swallowed by the trees along the winding track. Then she dropped off the bluff, Wolf beside her, and ran to kneel beside the injured woman.

Tatters of shirt hid the marks of the blows, but when Irene lifted the tail of it she saw that every bone in the woman's back must be shattered. Blood had smeared and spattered. A knob of vertebra showed between the shoulder-blades, and splinters of bone were visible in several places.

"Best she's dead, boy," Irene said to her dog. "She'd be a cripple or worse, if she'd lived. We'd better get help. Miz Goren, up the road, has a phone, I think. We'll go that way—it's a lot closer and faster."

She dropped the bloody shirt over the wreckage that had been a fairly pretty girl, and turned, holding the shotgun cradled in her arm. She reloaded, for who knew where that murdering bastard might be? It wasn't like the old days when the river was a place for family outings.

Then she set out up the red-mud track, keeping to one edge where pine-straw made for better footing. Wolf kept looking back toward the dead woman until they turned the first bend; then he shot ahead and out of sight, cutting across the woods. Irene felt a hundred and fifty by the time she caught up with him, but it wasn't far by then. Another quarter-mile and she'd be there.

The man, afoot now, came around the bend ahead. For an instant they were face to face, both shocked into silence. Then the burly fellow raised a pistol and took aim, at point-blank range.

Wolf shot forward, a sandy-red streak, and caught him by the elbow. The impact knocked the killer onto his back in the muddy road. Irene kicked the pistol into the woods and bashed the stock of the .410 against the side of the man's head. He didn't quite go out, but his eyes seemed to cock in different directions as she stepped around him.

"I could kill you," she said, "and nobody would question an old woman shooting a man she saw commit murder, but that would put me just about at your level. I'm not ready to go that low. So you stay put. I'm going to shoot out the tires of your truck, when I pass it, so don't think you can drive away." She turned her back, though she knew Wolf would growl a warning if he came after her, and trudged away. Behind her she could hear uninspired but fervent cursing.

It was no trick to spot his pickup, for it loomed above the young pines along the logging track where he'd tried to hide it. He must have intended to finish off the witness who'd shot at him. She shot out his front tires.

Before she tried to explain the situation to the Widow Goren, Irene made the call. She knew from long experience that the widow's combined deafness and senility would require many repeats of the story. Even then the old woman would get just about everything wrong. Still, it was little enough to give her some excitement to liven up her lonely days.

Much sooner than she expected, Cal Schneider, the local deputy, came screeching up in the Goren drive. "You call in a murder?" he yelled.

Irene got into the county car. "Right down beside the river. I saw it done, and I could have shot the man, but somehow I just couldn't. I did knock him in the head, which may have slowed him down some."

"I left him just about here," she said, as they came to the spot where a wallow in the mud marked the place where the man had fallen. "My dog kept him from shooting me, but it looks like he's run off into the woods. I plugged his tires when I saw his pickup back there on the logging track. It's still there, so he didn't even try for it."

Cal put the car in gear again and they crept down the ruts, coming to a halt when the limp figure came into view. "I won't get close—might mess up clues," he said.

"Clues be damned," Irene said. "I saw him beating her. Heard her scream way up at my place and came down the creek to see what was going on. He's a great big fellow, maybe six-two or so. Square beefy face with pale blue eyes—bloodshot, though that might be from drink or drugs, I guess. He had on dark blue jeans—looked new. Plaid shirt, blue and tan and gray, with a torn pocket on the left side. Oh, and he's got a brand new bruise alongside his forehead, shaped like a .410 butt.

"You can see his boot tracks right there along the riverbank. There's also a plain track on that poor girl's back, just above the hips." Irene figured that ought to do it, even for a slow thinker like the deputy.

Cal took a look at the girl's back and turned pale. "The Sheriff ought to be along pretty soon," he said. "I think I'll cover her up. Keep these damn flies off her a bit."

Irene nodded. Already bluebottles were buzzing and gnats were clustered in dark patches on the bloody spots. She wasn't terribly squeamish about such things, but Cal was young and still a bit tender, she thought.

"I'll sit on the stump here," she said. "You go and check on the radio. See if anybody can spot him crossing the road farther along toward the highway."

Gratefully, the boy took her advice, and she saw that his color improved. He was too young for this, she thought.

* * * * * * *

It was almost midnight by the time Cal dropped her off at her front steps. She had never seen so much activity—ambulance, paramedics, deputies, the sheriff stepping cautiously about in his snakeskin boots, though whether that was to avoid messing up evidence or to keep mud off those boots she was hard put to tell.

She'd gone into Talbot with the sheriff to give her statement, following the ambulance and the wrecker that was towing the murderer's pickup. She had described the murder in graphic detail, despite being just about tired to death by then. Her main worry had been whether Wolf found his way home all right, but he was waiting on the porch when she dragged herself up the steps at last.

Sheriff Cole had kept the .410 to test-fire, in case they needed to prove that the pattern of shot on the man's face matched it. Cal had secretly lent her the pump shotgun he kept in the back of his car, as it belonged to him. He also gave her a half-box of twelve-gauge shells, which rattled in her pocket as she clumped into the house and, for the first time in years, locked her door behind her.

Cal's words still echoed in her ears. "Miz Follett, that fellow's still around someplace close. You bein' alone like you are, I can't feel right if you don't have some protection. You keep a sharp eye out. Listen if your dog barks in the night too. That killer seen you close and plain. Lots of folks know what you look like, because your picture gets in the paper every time one of your paintin's sells for big money."

It had never occurred to her that the work she loved so well, which allowed her to live as she liked and where she liked, might betray her. She never bought newspapers. Though she was used to having interviewers find their way to her door, she never thought about what was done with all those notes they took or the cassettes they recorded as they asked their questions.

But if Cal, who knew as much about art as her dog, had seen her picture, then others had too. The thought made her cringe. She had always been a private person, and the thought of every Tom, Dick, and Harry in the county looking at her face and reading her words made her feel a bit sick.

Tonight, despite the heat, she must close and lock both doors. Not the windows—just as well be murdered in her bed as to suffocate there—but the doors had to be secured. Late as it was, she hated to take a bath, closed into the bathroom and unable to hear anything outside. She left the water running while she stood guard in the dark kitchen, and then she bathed quickly.

Before she went to bed she whispered to Wolf, who slept on the porch under her window, "You take care of things, Dog, you hear?"

His tail thumped the floor reassuringly, and she climbed into her bed feeling somewhat better. The shotgun leaning against the wall was also a comfort, and she drifted off quickly, exhausted by the trying day.

* * * * * * *

Wolf's growl brought her up from fathoms deep in sleep. Yet some part of Irene had stayed alert, even as she slept. She was up at once, the gun in her hands, her light cotton robe pocket bulging with ammunition belted around her pajamas.

She knelt beside the screened window. "Wolf?" she whispered. His tail thumped a reply, and his softest growl came again.

Something was out there, that was sure. If it had been a bobcat or an armadillo, he'd have been off that porch and after it like a streak. This was something he didn't quite know how to deal with; they'd lived together for twelve years, and she knew every sound he made as well as a mother knows her baby's cries.

Irene slid into her moccasins and moved down the hall toward the back of the house, avoiding creaky spots in the hardwood floor. The back door opened quietly—she hated squeaks and kept its hinges well oiled—and she slipped down the length of the back porch to step off behind the rose trellis. Wolf had worn his private trail all around the foundation of the house. She ducked low and used that as she moved toward the front. Before she reached her bedroom wall, she heard an incautious crunch as someone stepped too heavily onto the gravel of the drive.

Now Wolf was with her, though she hadn't heard him coming. His shoulder pushed against her hip as she crouched amid the bridal wreath and watched a dark shape moving toward the porch. She could feel the dog's heart beating—or was that her own?

It was very dark; only the fact that she had moved without turning on a light allowed her to see the black-on-black movement in her front yard. The steps squeaked; then he was on the porch. She could hear a chorus of warped and ancient boards moving under his weight.

The night cracked apart with noise as he kicked in the front door. "Old woman," he yelled, "I've come to git you! You think I done Estelle bad? Wait'll you see what I've got waitin' for you!"

His heavy steps moved into the central hallway; she heard him push open the living room door. Light splayed onto the porch as he found the switch, and she used its help to make her way silently to the broken door.

"I watched you come back," he shouted. "You'd as well come out as hide from me. No woman alive kin handle Ben Roswell, and you better not even try."

Irene thought of the woman at the river. She thought of his pistol, its muzzle staring into her face on the road. She waited just inside the door until he came back into the hall.

He was looking the other way, so she waited for him to turn to face her before pulling the trigger. A twelve-gauge pattern blossomed high on his chest as Ben Roswell sailed backward and fetched up against the hall tree.

Irene flicked the switch for the hall lights and stared down at him. His eyelids fluttered open and he stared up at her, his bloody jaw dropping. He tried to speak, but his throat and chest, lungs and heart were riddled with shot.

"Damn fool," Irene said. "A woman brought you into the world, and one can take you out of it. And good riddance."

Then she went to call the sheriff. He'd just have to come back all the long way to Bobcat Ridge and take away the carrion from her hallway.

Here's another story featuring Irene. You don't want to cross strange little old ladies!

THE TROTLINE

Although Irene Follett would rather sit and paint than do almost anything else, sometimes she found herself hankering to sit on the riverbank and fish for sun-perch. Today was one of those days, and she was having the dickens of a time making her inner vision of a terrapin, chewing on a leaf beside a creek, half hidden beneath fern, appear on the watercolor paper before her.

It was midsummer, and the heat was intense outside, although in her high-ceiled study the ceiling fan was doing a good job of keeping her cool. But the rich scent of pond water and fish and weed and snakes kept making her lose her concentration. Today was a fishing day, and that was all there was to it.

Being mid-week, there shouldn't be too many people on the river, she felt. Her favorite fishing spot, beneath a huge black gum tree, should be vacant. It was a long walk in such heat, and she decided to take her bicycle down the dusty sand and red clay road instead. Wolf, her half-red wolf dog, would love that too.

In fifteen minutes she had cleaned her brushes, washed her paint pans, and set the watercolor on the rack to dry. Fishing was in her blood and bones, and when that instinct called, she simply had to follow the urge. When she set out on her bike, she had her folding cane pole, a box of hooks and line, and a folding shovel in the basket behind her.

Wolf cocked his sharp ears, gave a gruff woof of approval, and ran ahead of her, flushing road-runners and other birds out of the ditches as he zigzagged forward. It was still early, and mockingbirds were giving enthusiastic concerts overhead, as she rode through the shady tunnel of arching branches.

She had been right—the river bank was empty of fishermen. Only an occasional plop, as big fish struck at the hovering damselflies in the middle of the river, interrupted the quiet. Irene unfolded her shovel, located a damp patch of dirt, and dug up squirming clots of fat red-gray worms. She kept only a half dozen; she had been raised never to waste anything, even earthworms.

Pinching one in half, she strung it onto her perch hook and leaned against the trunk of the tree. The bait dropped softly into the coffee-colored water, and the pine twig she used for a bobber began to dance regularly along the continual ripples. Eyes half closed, she watched the inverted shapes of the willows beyond the river make surreal patterns on the brown stream. Make a nice painting, she was thinking, when she glanced at her bobber, which was heading silently and swiftly downward at an angle. She pulled smoothly and a glittering perch swung high as she raised her pole.

Drat! Fishing for her was anticipating, not catching. She carefully freed the fish and returned it to the stream. Nice regular bites were what she liked, when she fished. Catching something interrupted her peaceful mood.

Overhead a long narrow bird the color of toast called, "Chiptwee! Stick it in your earrr!" and she smiled. Never heard that one before, that was for sure. Watching the birds was one of her primary reasons for coming.

There was a sudden *wump*, ending with a gigantic splash. Gator, she thought. In a moment another echoed the first.

Irene was beginning to get stiff by then, feeling all of her fifty-odd years in her joints. She rose, stuck the end of her pole deep into the mud, and wandered downstream, pausing to gather stiff bunches of purple ironwort as she went. Her hands filled with blossoms, she rounded the dog-leg bend and stopped, staring at two willows, one on either side of the river, that bent toward each other as if bowing.

"Sam Williams's trotline," she said aloud. "And I'll bet he's got a gator on it, the way those trees look." She whistled for Wolf, who came lolloping up, tongue dripping, his grin wide. Together they moved toward the nearer tree. Heavy cord strained downward from the loops securing it. She knelt, her experienced fingers freeing the knot, while holding the line fast. Then she walked along the bank, dragging the burdened line toward the shallows just upstream, though it was quite a struggle. There was something BIG on that line.

From the shelter of the willows, there came the boom of a gator's bellow. All this commotion should have scared any alligators away from the area by now. What held them here, when they should be moving away?

Then the weighted line dragged on the shelf of rock for which she had been heading, and she saw, tangled in the cord and looped with individual short lines and hooks, the body of a man. Through the mud and water weed she could see the unmistakable shade of a game warden's uniform.

"Thomas Lingard!" she gasped. There was a thorn bush near the edge of the water, and she secured her end of the line to it and stepped back to consider what to do. It would require at least half an hour to bicycle to her house. If she stopped at Mrs. Goren's cabin, a mile up the road, she'd take forever making the old woman understand. By the time she got back with help, alligators might well have taken off chunks of the poor fellow. It was best for her to wade out there and cut him loose, drag him ashore, and try to put him where gators would have a hard time dragging him into the river again. Once he was tucked under a root or a rock at the bottom, it would be a real job to find him.

Sighing with distaste, Irene pushed off her walking shoes, skinned off her socks, and put both on a stump. Then she moved slowly into the brown water, the mud squishing between her toes. The sharp edge of a mussel shell made her wince, and she felt her way cautiously around a bed of them, keeping always on a shallow shelf of rock. Below it the water became quite deep.

The blue-white face of the game warden turned upward as she cut the line beyond the body. Retching, Irene turned and towed the lax bundle ashore. The wet clay at the edge allowed her to skid him upward toward the stump where her shoes waited. When she examined the game warden carefully; gashes in both clothing and skin told her Lingard had been in the water only a short time. Otherwise the turtles and fish, as well as the gators, would have taken chunks of his flesh.

Irene glanced around, trying to find some safe spot to secure the remains. As she moved, a glint told her some vehicle was parked around the outthrust point of woods that ran down to the water. The old hunter's road that cut across the point would take a four-wheel drive vehicle like the warden's. That had to be his truck. Wrinkling her nose, she felt the right-hand pocket of the sodden uniform. Keys. Digging them out was no fun, but if she could get the truck over here, he'd be safe in its bed until she got back with a deputy.

The truck hadn't been there long, it was plain. When she backed it out of the nook where it was parked, the grass on which it had stood rose again before she had turned completely. Getting its owner into the vehicle, with her dog whining anxiously around her legs, was not something she recalled with any pleasure. She got the job done at last and sat on the stump to replace her socks and shoes.

Wolf knew something terrible had happened. The dog kept shivering and half whining, half barking, but when she whistled for him to follow her, he came after the bike.

Mrs. Goren wasn't at home. Two miles farther up the road the Stocktons were getting ready to drive to town when she panted into their front yard and stopped her bike beneath their huge umbrella chinaberry. "Got to make...a call!" Irene wheezed. "Body down there. At river. All right?"

Joyce Stockton was not a friend. The woman felt that any female who was not under the thumb of a man was somehow lacking in decency, particularly one who made for herself sums unheard of in East Texas, even for men. Now she looked at Irene as if she smelled as bad as the corpse would in a few hours. Still, nobody down here in the river bottom country would dream of turning down a neighbor in distress. She did look relieved when Irene asked her to make the call, not wanting her bedraggled clothing to drip mud and river water (if not worse things) in Joyce's tidy entry hall.

"Tell Sheriff Cole that I'll be down there just below the sharp bend. Where the rock shelf sticks out into the main current. He'll know," she told the woman. Then Irene sat on the brick edging of Joyce's front flowerbed and wiped her sweaty forehead on one sleeve.

"You're never going back down there alone!" Clark Stockton objected. "With a dead body?"

"He's not going to bother me," Irene said. "And if anybody else tries to, Wolf will scare him out of his socks."

"We'll go with you," the skinny man said, but even as he spoke he began to cough.

"This is your day to see Dr. Larkin," Irene told him. "I know that, and the doctor maybe can help you. He sure as hell can't help poor Lingard."

It took a lot of persuasion to get the Stocktons on their way to town. Then Irene rested for a while before tackling the ride back to the river. She was getting too old for this kind of shenanigans. Things kept happening down there at the river that never used to be heard about. Could be, she needed to get even farther away from civilization, if there was any such place. But she knew this was as far as you could get.

As she pedaled back along her trail, she thought of the last time she'd seen Tom Lingard alive. His job took him down the road often, and from time to time he'd stop at her house, drink a cup of coffee, and reminisce with her about the days when her father and his fished and hunted together in the big woods along the river. She sighed and stopped to rest again, propping her bicycle against a tree and leaning against it herself. She could see his big red face, alive with laugh wrinkles, as he told some particularly funny tale from the past. She was going to miss him, Irene thought, and no mistake.

She wondered which of the many illegal netters or poachers of deer might have killed him. Only last spring he had caught a bunch using illegal gill nets, and they'd burned his vacation cabin down on Lake Naconi. It must have been something a lot bigger and more dangerous that he'd found this morning. Or had the poachers found him?

With that in mind, she returned to the truck and drove it along the main trail into the woods until she reached the logging road that went back toward the giant magnolia tree at the edge of state land. If he wasn't where he was expected to be and anyone came checking on him, they might be puzzled enough to do something stupid.

He'd been moved already anyway, and when the sheriff's people came she could bring him back. Until then, she decided to take Wolf and hide in the shadows of the bluff overlooking the road and the river. She would have felt safer, of course, if she'd had a gun. There hadn't been a sidearm with the body, she had made sure. There wasn't a weapon inside the truck either. Well, she'd just have to do the best she could.

There was nobody there when she looked down on the shallows. The remnant of the trotline still bobbled from the tree on the far bank, trailing downstream. She found a spot layered with dead leaves and went flat. Wolf sat beside her, panting happily, as they waited. Ants crawled up her pants legs, mosquitoes zinged about her neck and face, but Irene was an old hand at watching in the woods. She never moved, and when there came the soft pad of feet on the sandy track below, she heard it.

It wasn't the law, that was certain. Nobody came down here afoot, in these days when folks didn't know what feet were made for. Irene focused her eyes and ears, blessing her good hearing, and waited for what might come next. She could feel her heart galloping in her chest, but that was excitement. Wolf's was too. She could hear it over his panting.

Three men and a woman came into view, slipping along through the brush, rather than walking the road. The woman stopped and pointed out over the river toward the tree where the rope still strained at its knot. "He might of hung up there," she said, and so intent was Irene that she made out the words.

"But it's broke," the tallest man said, his skinny neck craned to see. "S'pose a gator might of got him?"

"Could be." That was the old man, grizzled and grimy, who was staring too.

"Can't let him be found. If we could of kept him from fallin' in, we might of took him off to the other side of the county. If they find him here, somebody's goin' to remember how he got Pa sent up for gill-nettin' and moonshinin'. They're goin' to look spang at us, you wait and see." That was the third man, a wiry youngster who began wading out toward the trailing rope.

"You nitwit!" That was the woman. "Come back here! That water is twenty feet deep out there. You want to drown and keep Lingard comp'ny?" Even as she spoke, he slipped on something beneath the water, and the current took him out into the main stream. He evidently didn't swim well, for he began floundering and yelling, and his companions forgot their caution and yelled too.

Irene didn't wait. While they were distracted, she slid back through the trees to the truck, cranked it, and drove the long way around through the edge of a farm to come up on the spot again from the direction of town. She set the siren wailing, the lights flashing. (Tom had given her a ride once, and showed off all his bells and whistles.)

The group at the river's edge turned in dismay, saw the official truck heading toward them, and jumped like bullfrogs into the swift water of the Naconi River. Before any of them could reach the other side, there came another sound of a siren, and the sheriff's car pulled up with a screech.

"You, Irene," he yelled as she got out and moved toward him. "What you found now?"

"Better get those creatures first," she said. "Tom Lingard's body is in the back of his truck here. Those folks came to find the body. Said they'd lost it upstream, but they wanted to take it away someplace where nobody knew about their family's problems with the game warden."

Two deputies were already covering the dripping quartet as they found footing below the deep spot and splashed ashore. Irene sat on the stump where she'd put her shoes and watched the roundup.

"Sue Lee Grant," she said. "No 'count and never were. Moonshined with your daddy until he went to jail. Thurman Grant, timber thief. Arthur Grant, gill-netter and poacher. Caswell Grant, who ought to know better than to kill a law officer. You blasted idiots!"

She was so furious she didn't see, for a moment, Sheriff Cole's amusement. When she did, she stalked away to her bicycle and climbed aboard.

"Come on, Wolf," she snapped. "It's not enough that I do their job for them; they have to make fun of me too."

The dog cocked his head and stared up into her eyes. Then he turned and dashed after the Sheriff, setting his teeth firmly in his right pants leg and hanging there like a furry anchor while Cole dragged him forward two steps. "Irene, you get this animal off me," he commanded. "I swear, I'll have him picked up and put to sleep if you don't."

"Not unless you want a visit from me, you won't," Irene replied. "I'd have your Nettie on top of you like a duck onto a June bug. You don't take her only protection away from a helpless little old lady, now do you?"

Cole snorted, and Wolf loosed his grip and returned to her side, his furry tail wagging. As Irene pedaled away, she could hear the Sheriff's language, which was more than colorful.

When he cooled off, he'd come to the house to get her statement. Until then, she had her own business to attend to. She knew just how to finish that terrapin painting. She was going to add a trot-line across the stream behind him.

Families are a big deal in this neck of the woods. When you can't find enemies, sometimes family members will do...better!

YOU CAN'T GO HOME AGAIN

A swirl of oak leaves danced out of the wood across the road, and slapped pettishly at the windshield. For an instant, the cool October moon stared through their mottling shadows into my face. Then they blew on, and the road shone dimly in the glare of the headlights.

It was familiar, yet there was a difference. The sharp curve that my hands were braced for had turned into a gentle arc, banked to hold a car on the road. The uphill grade was cut down. I no longer would have had to shift into second to keep the engine from clattering, though my powerful Lincoln took any grade without a problem.

The cut that had lowered the road had left banks rising as high as the top of the car on either side. There it was dark, for the moon was still low, and it was early evening. At the darkest point, something pale and small flashed through the cone of light and was gone. A cat? Perhaps the umpteenth great-grandchild of the Angora that my mother had doted on and tormented?

Then I was at the top of the hill, looking out across clear space that had been thick stands of oak and ash and pine when I left home. The house shone in the moonlight, tall and commanding. Mama always resented the forest that hid her imposing home—she must have had it cut at last. I wished it back with all my heart, but the shorn meadow glimmered mockingly as the moon rose higher and the stars stared down. The house stared, too, from bleak, malicious windows.

I eased off on the gas, slid the lever into neutral. The car eased to a stop. How many years was it since I left that house behind? Almost thirty.... I had left my girlhood behind me, since last standing here. It was no rebellious nineteen-year-old who now returned to claim the heritage she never wanted and would never have possessed except for the deaths of two well-loved brothers.

Sitting there, sheltered from the pitiless moonlight, I thought of Ed and Vance. My big brothers, always sources of pride and frustration to me. Kind, off-handedly patient with my unfeminine presence, they bridged, to some extent, the hostile gap between my helpless smallness and Mama's powerful will. They meant me well, even while leaving me out of plans, ignoring my questions and comments—and me. I never quarreled with either of them, and now I was grateful for that. That unforgiving house could not charge me with disliking my brothers!

I shook myself from that dazed recollection. Fanciful notions, for one considering herself a skeptic! Now I owned that tall house, lock, stock, and barrel. I could burn it down, if I chose, for the insurance had lapsed while the lawyers tried to locate me to hand over this unexpected and unwanted heritage. They had had no cash to pay insurance or upkeep. There had been barely enough to bury Vance decently.

I smiled, thinking of the way in which my brother had enjoyed the wealth Dad had killed himself acquiring for Mama. He spent it to the last dime, and I was glad of it. I paid the lawyers' fees myself, and didn't begrudge a dime of it. I made more than enough, in the first half of my life, to entertain any fancy I chose during the last half, even if it meant a cash loss.

Making that success refuted, in my mind, Mama's assessment of me, which had been a mix of fury at my plainness, and frustration at my wrongheaded love of adventure and business. Before she died, I let her know, by way of Ed and Vance, that I had more than made good. Rags to riches described my career, though the rags had been Mama's idea, when I resisted her steamrollering of my life.

Not that Ed and Vance submitted to her. They had that easy grace that agrees tacitly with anything you say without betraying the fact that they intend to do whatever they damned well please when the time comes. I had been too honest—or perhaps pig-headed was the best word for it. Centuries ago, if I had been a boy, at the age of nineteen I would have sewn a cross on my cloak and found a Crusade to follow. I wanted conflict, challenge, a cause to give my life meaning. Mama gave me conflict enough, that was true, for we had been at daggers' points for a year when at last I left, dramatically and on foot, bearing my few possessions on my back in the best fairytale tradition.

I laughed, sitting there in the Lincoln and thinking of the night I walked down this road, the trees on either hand making dapples of moonlight across the gravel. I cranked the engine and eased forward toward the house. Then I was full of fury, determined to prove myself. Now I could only wish that someone was left who might care if I proved anything. My victory was empty.

The house was empty too. A daily cleaning woman had done for Vance, in contrast to the teams of servants who came and went under Mama's hard-handed rule. The daily maid had cooked for him, which was fortunate. If no one had invented pork and beans, Vance would have starved, if left on his own.

I drove around the circular drive and into the portico at the back. No limousine had ever pulled into its shelter to discharge important guests for a function over which Mama presided. If Dad had lived, it might have happened, but Mama was too impatient. She heckled him to his grave, I always believed, and by dying he only gave her more cause to complain.

I killed the engine and stepped out of the car. Sweeping away below, in all its splendor, was the view that Dad had found and built his house to enjoy. In the moon's chilly light, the forest stretched away, broken only by distant twinkles marking Gallatin, far to the north, and Venusia, almost below and fifteen miles away. Occasional sparks showed isolated farms. Mama always hated that view, which was the reason for her isolation from a world just waiting to worship at her feet.

My case was light. The bigger ones and the books I left in the car, as I unlocked the heavy door, whose stained glass inset was only a black glimmer in the darkness. The big brass key turned crankily, and the door swung open, letting me step, after so many years, into the impressive back corridor of my home. I shivered suddenly and touched the light switch.

Blast! I had sent money for the necessary connections, but the lawyers had not reconnected the electricity. I wondered suddenly if the oil tanks had been filled before Vance died. We were too remote for natural gas or any water supply except our own. If there was oil in the huge container in the cellar and water in the tanks on the roof, I might be able to survive until something could be done. The water pump to resupply the roof tanks would have to wait. I hoped the tanks had been filled recently.

I set my case in the hall and went to check the nearest bathroom. The tap turned stiffly, allowing a stream of water to run into the basin. It tasted a bit flat and galvanized (from the tank, of course), but the pressure was good.

The old lamps still should be in the kitchen, I suspected. Nothing ever changed in Mama's house, whether she was there or not. And sure enough, they sat on their high shelf, together with a two-gallon can of lamp oil. I set one on the kitchen table, and when it was lit, the mellow glow softened the clinical look of the room. I had always hated the kitchen, and so had all the cooks in the long roll of those who came to work for Mama. They usually lasted from a week to a month, as I recalled.

"It may be modern and sanitary," one had snorted at Mama upon leaving. "But it's like working in a confounded morgue. You can almost smell disinfectant!"

You still could, though it was obvious the place had not been scrubbed up thoroughly for a long time. I wondered suddenly about food.... I had been so distracted at the thought of coming here that I had never thought to pick up supplies.

I blessed Vance as I checked the pantry. Though the refrigerator and freezer were bare and clean, in the pantry shelves were row upon row of canned goods. An entire shelf of pork and beans took me back in time to our campouts—the rare ones that admitted a small sister to the complement. I could smell the smoke of the fire, taste the slightly ashy beans, the tin spoon—I brought myself back to the present with an effort. The second shelf held canned beef, vegetables of many kinds, soup, potato chips in cans. There was enough to do me well for as long as I wanted to stay, if I didn't become too weary of canned food. I had never been even as much of a cook as Vance.

The house was cold, chilled with the damp of an unoccupied house in late fall. I tried the furnace, pumped the pilot—then remembered that the fans required electricity. Knowing my Mama, I knew the old oil heaters were probably in the cellar, beside the new furnace. I felt certain that there would be enough oil left in the tanks, even unfilled ones, to fill one for days. Those big tanks had never been completely empty in all the years I lived here.

It took a lot of bumping and swearing, but at last I got the bulky heater into the library. There I cursed the lack of care that left Dad's valuable books to the mercies of damp and insects. I brought a couple of the lamps, as well, and when all were alight, the room began to warm, and the light chased away unwelcome memories.

I cleaned up in the nearby bath—in cold water, of course—put on my flannel pajamas and my woolly robe, and returned to sit in the deep chair that Mama had consecrated to Dad's memory. I had never sat in it once in my entire life. Her smaller armchair was set at an angle beyond the marble topped table holding the lamp. I could almost see her there, her gray hair tied into an uncompromising knot, her black eyes snapping as she charged me with some unforgivable sin that no proper daughter would ever dream of committing.

I closed my eyes for a moment. Then I stared around the room. The fireplace was sealed, as it had been since Mama put in the furnace ("inefficient!" Mama had said). The mantel was still filled with delicate jade sculptures, which had been Ed's treasures. I ached suddenly, seeing his big brown face, his huge hands tenderly cradling one of the pieces.

On the library table were Vance's sailing ships, twenty-five of them, each the product of months or even years of work. Some he carved from ivory he found in antique shops, some he made of woods, and some of filigreed metal. All were lovely and fragile—as gossamer as Vance had been tough and square-hewn.

I had seemed to be the gentle, sensitive one, but inside I was tough and determined. Of the three, I was the only one to tackle and conquer the giant Money. I sighed.

Something moved at the edge of the pooled lamplight. Pale and furry, it looked like...a cat? But the house had been empty for months. How could one have survived without help and alone?

Mama's Angora had borne me no malice. Indeed, it had cuddled in my lap, when we could find a private moment free of Mama, before she called "Ginni! Ginni! Where has that cat got to?" and that sent the animal scampering. She, too, knew the penalty of crossing Mama.

"Kitty-kitty!" I called. I felt foolish. How could there possibly be a cat here?

There was no sound, no hint of motion. I settled back in Dad's chair and looked in the direction I'd been avoiding all evening. Mama's portrait, hanging over the long table, had been painted by the foremost painter of her day, at the height of her early beauty. She had believed with all her might that her talented husband was going to pull her, along with him, to the height of social and political power.

Even I could see that she was lovely then, though to my knowing eye the beginning of the domineering curl had already touched her smiling mouth. There was the hint of hardness in the dark eyes. Yet she seemed, there in oils, all grace, tenderness, and beauty. I used to come into this room, as a child, to look at the picture and to wonder what fairy had stolen away that lovely woman and substituted the mother I knew. The contrast between the person the artist had seen and what that woman had become still puzzled me.

She had great determination. Her talents varied from a competence in business to a genius at manipulating people. Why had she not gone out, after Dad died, and used his wealth and her wits to make her own place in the world? I had been too young to wonder, at the time, but I did so now.

Then I shuddered. Something touched my ankle, and I stared down into an inquiring Angora face. Smiling, I scraped the remnants of my corned beef onto a saucer and slid it beneath the chair, wondering how the beast had survived. The mouse population must be down to nothing—and how had it gotten water? Then I recalled the toilet in the bathroom.

Its lid was open.

I didn't watch, for Ginni had hated being observed when eating. Instead, I rose and took my dirty plate and cup back to the kitchen. Nothing could have made me leave it until morning, for Mama might return from her grave to call me a slob.

The hall was lit dimly by the lamps in the library as I returned, picking my way between small Persian rugs. I froze in place as a voice called from above, "Ginni! Ginni! Where has that cat got to?"

The shrill tone scraped along my nerves. My ears rang with it. Suddenly I recalled what Ed had written me, shortly after Mama's death. "We knew for some time that she was failing. You remember Ginni, the cat? She still had an Angora, this one called Ginni too. Three days before she died, Mama called in Dr. Allison and asked him point-blank if she was dying. He didn't try to deny it.

"After he was gone, she called Ginni and Vance and me into her room. We thought she was going to say goodbye—give us some sort of last instructions—maybe ask us to find you. At least something that normal people do when they die. Not Mama. She strangled the cat and handed it to me.

"'Go bury it in the garden'," she said. And I did, but I have to admit that for the first time I realized that you were right about Mama. I suppose my memories went back to when Vance and I were little, and she was still a human person. Now I know why you left, Berna. I understand a lot of things. I'm going to move away, for I can't seem to bear it here any more."

He did leave, and he died four years after that, though he was only thirty-six at the time. Vance had shared Mama's money with him freely, but he didn't enjoy it, and he just drifted away in Mama's wake.

Now I was in the hall where I had stood so many times, hearing her call her cat. That small sad shape in the library—was it or was it not a living animal? I hurried into the room and looked under the chair. The saucer of food had not been touched, though a long pale hair clung to the upholstery of the flounce edging the slipcover.

The voice came nearer, as if Mama were coming downstairs. "Ginni!"

My hand touched something under the chair, soft and tenuous. Almost not there, yet tangible. I closed my fingers about the furry shape, and something not quite invisible came into the light with my hand. There was the ghost of a purr.

I stood, feeling my knees shake beneath me. I felt myself turn pale, and I had to admit that I was cold with terror. I had feared her alive. How could I face her dead? The thing in my hand squirmed about, as if trying to hide against me.

I spent years in trying to escape from the house and Mama. I had achieved the impossible again and again, believing that it would free me from her. But it had not. Tucking the cat beneath my arm, I stepped forward and kicked over the stove, spilling blazing oil over the Persian carpet. I thought of the books—a pity, but necessary.

In the hall, I caught up my case and my purse. My jacket came out of the closet, with the keys of the car in a pocket. I went quietly and not too quickly down the hall toward the rear entry. There came a screech behind me. "You! Berna! I always knew you were no good! Where's my cat? Ginni! Don't take her away!"

I was at the door, leaving it open behind me to the rising breeze. The car started with the ease of expensive engineering, and I pulled around the circle and down the drive. Where the woods had been, I stopped and stepped out to watch the house burn. It was like a beacon. They would see it in Gallatin. Trucks might well come up from Venusia, but they would be too late. Mama and her house were going up in flames.

Would I be free at last? I was taking with me something, not a living, visible creature, but something that had feared Mama as much as I had. I saved Ginni, at last, from her murderer. Something in that act also saved me. Maybe now I could go on and live a life, find someone to share the rest of it. Make two or three more fortunes?

The wind freshened in my face. The cold October moon shone overhead. Against my chest there was the tremulous hint of a purr.

We don't lack for criminal types in the piney woods. There has been more than one bank robber or murderer lost forever in our woods, fields, and old abandoned houses. And even now bodies turn up in the oddest places. Too often the killers are never found....

HIDEOUT

The stout walls, built of heart-pine, had been under attack by weather and insects for a decade. The roof had begun to sag, and the porch steps were a sift of sawdust left by the invading termites. Hawthorn and privet bushes had run wild, and berry vines had thrust questing fingers into every possible crevice.

Only dust moved inside, except for an occasional roach and the omnipresent spiders in the corners. Even vandals and couples looking for a place to make out did not go there.

What had happened ten years before had left its mark on the minds of locals, and it was not the sort of matter that country people can forget.

The furniture was still in place, veiled with cobweb and dust, for not even a thief had entered the place. An occasional breeze, gusting through broken panes, fluttered the webs, shaking down more dust that danced in the sun rays slanting through cracks in the walls.

It didn't seem likely that anyone would ever come there again.

* * * * * * *

Harper felt the impact of the slug even before he realized he had heard the shot. It knocked him sideways into a tangle of sawvine, which was lucky for him and fatal for Seldane. He rolled to come up on his belly, the revolver bulky in his grip. As Seldane looked over the bush behind which he had taken cover, Harper shot him through the head.

The sharp echoes died away into the woods, and he knew that

nobody was nearer than five miles who might hear them. For the first time since they had pulled the bank job two hours ago, he was safe. And now the money was his, all of it. It was only right—he hadn't been the one to try to backshoot his partner.

Blood was sticky in his shirt—he was hit just below his left armpit, but the bullet had angled away from his chest. It seemed to have torn a hole in the muscle as it exited the wound, but he knew what to do about that. Korea had taught him a lot, and 'Nam had finished his education. He tore up his shirt and packed it into the worst of the holes, reducing the bleeding, as far as he could tell, to a minimum. Once he thought he wouldn't bleed to death, he crawled out of the vines and went to examine Seldane. The briefcase lay beside him in the pine straw—forty thousand dollars was inside it, still undivided, and now not to be. All his.

Small banks might not keep millions of dollars on hand, but they didn't have much security. On balance, they made far better marks than bigger, richer banks did.

He hadn't begun to hurt yet, though his head felt a bit light and the wood was tilting a bit from time to time. He hefted the briefcase in his good hand, after stuffing the gun into his belt. He followed the dim path that was supposed to lead to the spot where Seldane had stashed the second car. The first was ditched in a ravine, several miles behind off a logging road.

Harper felt a tiny regret that he no longer had Seldane to guide him through the forest. This was his partner's neck of the woods—he knew the trails through the thickets as only a native country boy could, and already Harper was feeling confused. He came to a fork in the path. Each track, leading into the shadows of the trees, looked equally abandoned and unpromising. He couldn't recall Seldane's mentioning a fork, and he certainly hadn't expected to need such information. Now he had to choose.

"Eeny-meeny-minie-mo," he chanted aloud. His voice sounded odd, and he thought he must be feeling the wound and the blood loss more than he suspected. He turned right, through a stand of hickories. The path slanted down toward a creek that ran through gray-barked birches and ranks of cattails. He sloshed through the water, feeling mud ooze into his loafers, and smelling the thick greenish stink of stagnant muck. Seldane had said nothing about a creek!

The light grew dimmer, and he shook his head to clear his vision. Then he realized that the sun was getting low beyond the thick stands of pine and hickory and oak. Straight up, the sky was still bright, but in the forest it was already twilight.

The path ended in a swamp. Button willows leaned over green

pools, and cypresses that seemed too fat to be healthy thrust their trunks and knees up from the ooze. He'd been following a logging track! But where was the back road where the car was waiting?

He began to sweat—or was it blood soaking through the packing and trickling down his skin? He turned and hurried along the path to find the fork. It was even darker, as he took a turn onto what he hoped was the right track. In two hundred yards, he emerged onto a dirt road, barely one vehicle's width, whose ruts were almost grown over with weeds.

God! He had been afraid he would miss it! But where was the car? There was no parallel track among the overgrowth—it had to be farther down the road. Right? Left?

He went right for some distance, with no result. Then he retraced his steps and went the other way. Nothing. Where was the damned car?

Now it was really getting dark. He was also becoming weak and dizzy. He had to find someplace to hole up for the night. Stumbling around blindly would never get him to the car. He staggered along, brushing through the bushes that were trying to lean across the track. But up ahead he saw a break in the row of trees and brush. Though the sun was down, streaks of pink and orange still hung in the west, and he could just see the glint of rosy light off a tin roof. The break was a driveway, though weeds and vines had grown over it.

An empty house. Just what he needed!

He stepped into the brambles, trying not to leave too plain a trail. He had no doubt that deputies and what-not would be searching the countryside in the next few days. Probably they'd have choppers and dogs. He had seen it before, though never from the wrong end of things.

It was too bad he hadn't found the car. He could be out of the state before the law got its act together. That was why he and Seldane had picked a town so near the Louisiana line for this operation.

He found that things were going hazy. He was suddenly on hands and knees in the stickery mass that was the drive. As it seemed too much trouble to walk, he crawled, though it was murder on his hands. Things kept going into and out of focus, as he struggled toward the house. In one of his lucid moments, he realized that he was in trouble, but the thought wouldn't stay with him. He sighed and forced his way forward, stopping only when he butted into the sagging sill of the porch. When he opened his eyes it was darker, but he was staring into the total blackness beneath the house. A stone block held up the corner of the porch, and he used it to pull himself up, after heaving the briefcase onto the flimsy planking.

The boards sagged. Dead leaves and grit rustled beneath him, as he moved toward the gaping doorway. A sawvine had sent a runner over the porch and into the open door, and he had to push aside the stickery tangle before he could get inside.

It was like going into a cave. The last of the light from the sky was gone, and before he knew that furniture still cluttered the room, he bumped himself sharply. "Got to have light," he muttered, holding onto his wits with difficulty. "See...what's...what."

The room was a mess. His lighter was all but out of fluid, and the space was only a dim cave. Cobwebs criss-crossed it, and chairs were tumbled this way and that as if there had been a free-for-all there before it was abandoned. Something scuttered in a corner, invisible in the blackness.

"Not a good place for a sick man," he said. "Feels like a tomb. A blasted tomb." The words echoed through the invisible rooms.

He hauled himself upright, holding onto the heavy armchair he had bumped last. The room was full of bulky shapes. Why hadn't people taken what they wanted from this house?

He stumbled forward, found a mantel. It was thick with dust, but his seeking hands found a candlestick, with a length of candle left in it. Dusty strands dripped from the wick, but he flicked his lighter and lit it. It sputtered and smoked, trails of sparks running down the threads of web, but it caught well at last. The tiny light seemed very bright, after the unsteady flicker of the lighter.

Harper set his briefcase of money on the sofa sagging beside the fireplace. He looked around, finding that a table at the back of the room still held dishes, set as if for a meal. If people had left in such a hurry, he realized, they might have left canned goods in the kitchen.

He lifted the candle and moved toward the door at the back of the room. A strip of something was draped across the table holding the dishes—a streamer with printing on it:

KEEP OUT

POLICE CRIME
INVESTIGATION IN PROGRESS

He shivered. Something really nasty had happened here. There had been a body. He had seen strips like that out in the woods, when corpses had been found and the law had searched.

But solid country folks didn't have such things happen. Surely someone had found this strip and brought it home as a curiosity.

He stumbled into the other room, a kitchen with an old-fashioned tin sink. A dish cupboard stood to one side, and inside the wire-covered upper shelves were more dishes and glasses. Another door opened to the side...a pantry, he hoped.

There were empty bags on the floor, covered with dust and issuing a moldy smell that told him potatoes and onions had rotted away there. There were also shelves along the walls, and on them were jars. One entire wall was filled with full ones, though the contents of some were covered with mold.

He picked through them, peering closely in the light of the candle. Pickles. Still green—all that vinegar should have kept them in good shape. Another jar held something dark red, without mold. Beets. More vinegar—safe too. Peaches, warmly golden under the dusty glass. Fig preserves, dark but always good.

He felt his knees wobble. This was no balanced meal, but it would have to do. He had lost too much blood, and he needed some kind of food to keep him going. After tomorrow, he would have forty thousand reasons to eat well and sleep in comfort.

He opened the jars in the kitchen. Peaches first—the juice was sweet, and he could feel the juice building energy. Figs. A pickle or two. He found himself swaying dizzily before he was done.

But he explored a bit more, though he found himself inexplicably unwilling to cross the dog-run into the other half of the house. Even if there were beds there, he didn't want to sleep in one. Now that he had something inside him, he found that he had a chilly feeling when he wondered what had happened here.

He looked about at the walls, whose plain boards were covered with tatters of newspaper. The sink was corroded, filthy with dust and mouse-dirt. There were smears of something dark on the floor, under the litter. Something brown and thick had spilled there, long ago.

He pushed aside the bits of newspaper and accumulated trash and stared down. There was a big blotch, and beside it was a chalk-mark, shaped like a body lying on its side, arms extended, legs drawn up. He found himself shaking again. The candle fluttered as he turned to leave the kitchen. He would burn furniture in the front room, make a fire in the fireplace. He wanted lots of light!

He found himself weaker than he thought, and it was with some difficulty that he broke up a couple of chairs and set them alight, using newspaper stripped from the walls. But he was done at last, and when the fire was going merrily, heating the room entirely too much, he settled onto the couch in front and ran his fingers through his money.

Something chittered overhead—he jerked nervously before he told himself that it was a bat in the attic. There were mice all over, according to the droppings, and who knew what else, here in the woods. He must not let himself become nervous. He had to keep from getting weak, though his head kept trying to float away into another dimension.

He fell asleep on the sofa, as the fire burned itself out. Night filled the rooms, as it had done without interruption for a decade. The house endured everything, even this new encroachment that had come to haunt it with problems other than its own. When Harper woke, he was covered with cold sweat. He felt as if a cold mist surrounded him, touching his fevered skin, weighing on his chest. He stared into the darkness, straining to see, but the candle had burnt out and the fire was dead.

Some sense he hadn't known he possessed was hearing noises from the kitchen. A crashing, followed by a shriek, mouse-thin but audible to his interior ear. A struggle, moving through the house, across the dog-run into the bedrooms, back into the parlor where he lay, stiff with terror. Blows were struck by nothing, hitting nothing, yet they could be heard by anyone there to listen.

Harper tried to roll off the couch, as the terrible conflict came near. But he had been bleeding for hours, and he was too weak to move. He could do nothing, as the sounds filled his mind. He clenched his fists, closing his eyes and moaning. This was delirium. It had to be. He was seriously hurt—or it might be something in the canned stuff he had eaten. He was hallucinating, and daylight had to see the end of it.

Something touched his cheek, moth-soft. Chilly. There was another blow, crashing into his mind as devastatingly as the slug had crashed into his body, and he knew nothing more.

* * * * * * *

The sun rose calmly, sending streaks of light through chinks and splits, making dust-motes dance in the room, as they had done for years. The house was still, as usual, resisting with all the strength of heart-pine the encroachments of termites and ants and dry-rot.

Inside, the ants, with their excellent intelligence work, had found the body and were marching solemnly into and out of the wounds, checking out the ears and the nostrils, making a long safari up the tongue. A beetle was sitting on a glazed eyeball, taking some sort of esoteric delight in its position.

The dust was settling over the chalk-marked kitchen floor, covering up old bloodstains and new man-tracks. The vines in the drive had already sprung up to hide any trace of someone's passing.

The searchers' cars passed and repassed the old driveway, as the lawmen cast about for traces of their prey, but nobody looked into that long-empty house.

Not even a bank-robber would be foolish enough to go there, they knew.

Bird Hunting is a popular sport around here. I grew up in a hunting family, and one of the setter pups was my "brother" for years. I have run the fields with the dogs and when about three, walking in the woods with my mother, my dad, and the setter bitch, I came down in a point. The dog backed me, and my dad went forward and kicked up a covey of quail. I may have missed my calling—might have been a champion bird dog. However, sometimes a dedicated hunter might go to real extremes to get in an afternoon of hunting....

DOWN IN THE BOTTOMLANDS

I'd been warned that it would be rough going, but being young and hard-headed, I put on my brand-new hunting boots, took my brand-new shotgun out of its case, and loaded my brand-new English setter into the car. We started off in high spirits, for I'd been told that partridge were thick as fleas in the Nichayac River Bottoms.

That was where I wanted to hunt. The codgers who had warned me about the brush and the sawvines were short on wind and heavy on their feet. I could go where they couldn't, I knew. I was young and strong and eager, and they were just old poops.

I found my way fairly easily, but I ran out of road several miles before I got to the bottoms themselves. That didn't surprise me—in East Texas you can run out of roads and a lot of other things, when you get down into the boondocks. I've met old nesters, out on my rounds selling cattle feed, who still use kerosene lamps for light, and a well and privy for conveniences.

A good few of those look as if they never have come out to see what the twentieth century looks like. But a lot of the old ones have died in the past few years. Now their gray board-and-batten houses sit in the woods and the abandoned fields, melting back into the red dirt among rampant berry vines.

I stopped my car at the end of the road, beside just such a house. Beyond was a cow-trail leading off into brush. Old Rock, my setter, bounced out of the car as soon as I opened the door and began sniffing around the jungle that used to be a yard.

I loaded the gun and put on my hunting vest and jacket, feeling to make sure my extra ammunition and my lunch were in the proper pockets. Then we set off along a path Rock found, which soon led us into a cornfield that was a perfect hell of broken-over stalks tied together with bindweed and more berry vines. I began to understand what the old fellows meant by rough going.

Beyond the field, we found cut-over woods. It was an obstacle course of discarded treetops and sawvines and young huckleberry and hawthorn. Rock was nosing around, his tail quivering the way it did when he smelled birds, but he didn't find a covey. It was perfect territory for quail, but we worked our way through it without raising anything but a big hawk.

By then I was sweating. It was a damp, cloudy December day, chilly at the beginning but warming up later. I took off my jacket and tied it around my waist. I could feel sweat around the band of my cap, and the walking didn't get any easier at all. The new boots were chewing up my feet by then too.

Then Rock hit a pretty fair path, a nice foot-wide trail leading right through the tangled mess. A crow called overhead, and I looked up, trying to see him. By that time I was in a stand of young pine and couldn't, but I paused and listened. There wasn't another sound, after the caw died away. Not a chickadee or a cardinal ate seeds in the brush. No woods-noise could be heard, even the ones so regular and natural that you don't realize you're hearing them.

It was spooky. I whistled to Rock, and he crashed through the brush to my side. I was glad of the noise—all that quiet was really lonesome.

The deeper we went, the quieter that patch of woods got. If I hadn't hated the thought of going back through that cornfield, I might have turned around and gone home. But by then my feet were like hamburger. They tried to tell me about wearing new boots for an all-day hunt, but I was too bull-headed to listen. Now I had to find a place to sit down and take them off, come what might.

So we went on, following the path. Rock pattered ahead of me, not even trying to sniff the undergrowth. I could see by the way his ears twitched that the silence was getting to him too.

It was almost noon by then. I was ready to stop and eat lunch and get those boots off, but you never in your life saw a place as likely to hold copperheads as that woods. There wasn't even a stump or a rock to perch on. By the time I was ready to plump down in the middle of the path, we came around a clump of huckleberries and found ourselves looking at a house. You might not have called it that—shed, maybe. I've seen smokehouses that were solider.

The yard was scraped clean down to the sand, which told me that an old-timer lived there. Pock-marked slop jars sat along the porch, holding frost-killed plants. Whitewashed tires held what had been ferns, and big bunches of herbs hung from the porch roof. Everything was neat as a pin, though almost ready to fall down. I stopped at the fence and called, for out here that's the safe and polite thing to do.

Something was cooking. Well, maybe that isn't the right term for it. I smelled something, which didn't make the mouth water but definitely was steaming. I felt certain my peanut butter sandwiches would be much better, and I hoped the owner of the shack wouldn't ask me to lunch.

A step inside made the porch roof wobble. The doorway was filled completely with a huge man. He stepped out onto the porch and looked down from the three-foot elevation. Some six and a half feet of his own put his head over a yard above my own. I felt like a pigmy.

"Howdy," he said. He waited for me to take up the conversation.

I stepped into the yard and said, "Hello. My name's Wilson Clevenger, and I've been bird hunting. Back there." I waved back toward the woods. "Would you mind if I sat on your steps to eat my lunch? It looked too snaky to risk it, back in the trees."

He moved onto the rickety steps. They sagged alarmingly beneath what must have been nearly three hundred pounds. "Full of copperheads," he agreed. "Not safe to sit. Mighty nigh not safe to walk either. Not without good new boots like yours. Sit. Water?"

"Thank you." I had a thermos of coffee, but to refuse hospitality with these woodsy people wasn't polite.

I ate my sandwiches and drank clear, cold water from his well, which tasted faintly of the cedar bucket holding it. I threw in a comment, now and again, and he gravely tossed back a monosyllable of reply. As I finished, he sighed. "Been a long time since I been able to hunt. Gun's wore out. Dog died. I'm too heavy to get around. Used to love to hunt." He stared at me, his head tilted as if sizing me up.

"It's a young man's sport," I said. "My Dad used to go every year, but once his legs went out on him he couldn't do anything but give me advice."

He rose from his perch on the edge of the porch. "You got to have some of my brew," he said. "Been wanting company, and sure enough, the minute I get it finished, here you come. It don't taste near as good when you drink it by yourself."

I didn't want anything he had cooked up, particularly if it was moonshine, and most particularly if it was the stuff I could still smell. But it isn't polite (or safe) to refuse such an offer. Not from someone who would make two and a half of you. I smiled and reached for the cup he brought from the shack. The taste surprised me. Not bad at all, it was even a bit alcoholic. It tasted sort of greenish, too, but spicy. Its heat made me sweat, and the breeze cooled me down considerably.

"Not bad," I said, handing the cup back.

He grinned like a jack-o'-lantern. "Just the ticket to put you in shape for hunting. There's a covey down toward the river. Been keepin' an eye on them all fall. You just sit back while I put on my beat-up old boots, and I'll show you where to go."

The way my luck had been running, I couldn't turn down his offer. I called Rock and sat back, leaning against a porch post. My eyes seemed very heavy, and I yawned. I relaxed....

* * * * * * *

When I opened my eyes again, the sun was just about to go down behind the woods to the west. Rock lay at my feet, looking tired to the bone. My gun leaned beside me, smelling like powder, as if it had been shot again and again. I shook my head and sat up.

"What in the name of...?"

My host stepped to the door. "You sure did have a spell of good luck," he said. "Thanks for the mess of birds—you didn't have to do that. I was glad of your company. You was welcome to hunt my land."

I shook my head, and it felt as if all my brains had come loose and were jangling around like the works of a broken clock. As I moved, I felt weight in the bird pouches of my hunting vest. Reaching back, I felt feathers. A lot of feathers.

"How many did I get?" I asked. I couldn't recall ever rising from my seat on the step.

"An even dozen. I'll savor the four you gave me. It's been a long time since I got quail and gravy. You best be starting back, though. Gets hard to find the way in these woods at night. Wouldn't want you getting lost."

I rose hurriedly. My feet felt even worse than they had when I sat down with the gun and my dog. My legs ached. As I hefted the shotgun, I found my shoulder painful from the kick of the twelve-gauge. No way could I have slept through firing a shotgun!

Rock rose wearily, as I stood looking up at the elderly giant on the porch. "Enjoy your birds," I said, in as innocent a tone as I could manage.

The wrinkles at the corners of his eyes deepened, as he grinned. A faint hint of the smell of that brew still lingered in the air, and I could detect its aftertaste in my mouth.

The sun eased under a layer of cloud, and the woods stood still as death around us. "Don't take too long in the woods," he said. "Things come out at night, you know."

I didn't want to know. Without another word, I turned on my painful feet and forced my bone-weary legs away from that falling-down cabin into the dusky wood. An owl hooted behind, as we crossed the pine woods and plunged through that hellish cornfield. We made it to the car just before full dark.

You can't speed much on a washboard dirt road. That's probably a good thing, for I was shaking too hard to steer competently.

I had it figured out, finally. He hadn't just borrowed my gun and my dog for his evening's hunt. He had borrowed me!

I doubted I'd ever hunt partridge again. Particularly not in the Nichayac Bottoms.

It's an odd life for anyone of any color in East Texas. If you're black and a woman, it can be terrifying....

LONESOME CANEFIELD BLUES

"It's too hot to breathe," sighed Hibiscus, fanning hard with the ancient cardboard advertising piece that a long-dead snuff salesman had given her grandmother a generation before. The wicker handle, which had been re-stapled many times to the faded fan, wiggled dangerously as she waved it.

"Old High-Biscuits found somethin' she can't handle?" her sister asked from her perch on the porch steps. "Thought you could do great things and catch wild cucumbers, since you finished that Yankee college. You don't mean this little old hot spell has got you down?"

Hibiscus sighed again, more deeply. She'd thought nothing could be worse than staying here, working in the cane fields, probably marrying Jim, and never learning anything about the world. But now she had caught a glimpse of what existed beyond the fields. Tantalized by her reading and the trips she managed to make to New York and Boston and Philadelphia, she hungered for more.

Sunny, however, had never needed or wanted to see anything farther off than the county seat or more complicated than the Saturday night dances at the community center. Her sister was not the material from which scholars were made, and that was dandy. She was just where she wanted to be.

Yet Hibiscus, newly graduated Magna Cum Laude from a prestigious New England college to which she had earned a full four-year scholarship, found herself tied again to the tenant house and the rented farm. Her brand new wings were drying and shriveling, never having been allowed to unfold in the air of the academic world.

There came a groan from inside the house. She rose hurriedly and went into the kitchen, taking a bowl of cold water from the rusty refrigerator, a cloth from the line strung from cupboard to corner.

An air conditioner would have been such a mercy to her father.

She pushed the thought away and went to wash his sweaty face. The sheets were sweaty too, and she changed them after she washed his wasted body, which was taking so very long to die.

"Pearlie?" His eyes were trying to focus on her in the dim light of his shuttered room. "Pearl?"

"Yes, Baby, yes," she crooned, though her mother had been dead for a decade.

"You just take your medicine and go back to sleep, Daddy. You'll feel better directly." She took the vial of painkiller Doctor Barry had given her and held it up to the light. There were maybe three doses left. Would he give them some more or would she have to leave Sunny in charge of Daddy and go back to the fields to make enough to buy it?

She took the needle from the aluminum pan, shook the water from the barrel, and put the thing together. By the time she gave her father the shot, he was ashy-blue with the pain. He needed to be in the hospital, she knew, but there was no money, no insurance, and he wasn't old enough for government help.

She cleaned the needle again and put it to boil on the propane stove for precisely five minutes. The extra heat in the tiny kitchen almost made her feel faint.

The porch felt relatively cool when she returned to it. The sun was all but down. The shadows of the trees along the creek reached long fingers toward the paintless house. Sunny was sitting on the step, her blue-flowered cotton skirt swirling out around her creamy brown legs, giggling at some thought in her pretty, empty head. "George says he goin' to marry me!" she said casually. Her slanted eyes sparkled as she looked sideways at her sister. "Ain't goin' to have him, no way, no how!" She giggled. "But he sure is mad. I told him Sat'day, and he didn't like it even a little bit."

Hibiscus, sitting again in the creaky swing, straightened, feeling a dim alarm. George was huge and jealous-hearted. When he got mean-crazy, he could be dangerous. She had known, when Sunny kept leading him on, that the girl was asking for trouble, but that was Sunny's problem now. She had all she could handle with Daddy.

Sweat trickled down her back and her arms and beneath her breasts. The heat, instead of declining, seemed to be intensifying. It was enough to drive you crazy, without worrying about anything else.

She listened—Daddy's breathing was quiet and even, his pain submerged in a tide of painkiller. Yet, beyond that familiar sound, there was another. Someone was walking on the grass outside the fence. She rose and went into the house. She was in no mood to make small talk with anybody. Not tonight.

The sound of the cane-knife hacking into flesh shocked her still. There couldn't be any mistake. She'd heard it once before, when she was ten and Big Eddie had gone crazy and killed his wife right there in the field where the family had been working. Hibiscus grabbed the hog-killing knife from its rack and moved toward the porch.

Sunny was on the porch. Hibiscus felt her panic ease—what could she have heard? Then she saw a bare foot, its pale sole upward, beyond the last step. She was beside Sunny in one convulsive leap.

The cotton dress was now patterned with scarlet poppies among the pale blue cornflowers.

She heard the sound again, this time from inside the house. From the bedroom.

"Daddy!" she shrieked. She was answered by a laugh, quiet and amused. It was more frightening than anything she could recall since that terrible summer when she was ten and Big Eddie killed his wife.

Without pausing, she ran as hard as she could toward the cane field beyond the creek. Once inside the eight-foot barrier of stalks and knife-edged leaves, she might be able to elude any pursuer. The hog knife was no match for a cane knife in length and breadth, not to mention lacking the wicked hook on the leading edge. Still, it was better than nothing.

She cleared the creek in one leap, startling a spatter of frogs into the water, protesting and yelping. A water moccasin slid away before her pounding feet. She shivered, remembering how many snakes usually hunted the cane fields at night.

The field came almost down to the line of trees along the creek. She tore into the thick growth, and in three strides her skin was a network of tiny cuts from the leaves. Her hands went up to shield her eyes, and she looked down past her palms to the ground where her feet must land. To step on a moccasin now was to suffer a worse death than even George could inflict.

She had cut cane in this field all her life. She knew every hummock, every hollow. She knew the place on the far edge where the crop always grew so thickly that it was almost impossible to find room to swing a cane-knife to cut the stalks. If she could wriggle into that jungle of plants, deep in where you couldn't walk and could hardly crawl, she might escape George's notice.

She was all but sliced to ribbons by the time she crossed the field. Her dress hung in tatters around her, and her arms and legs streamed blood from the cuts and scratches. She dropped into a panting heap at the place where the cane grew too heavy to penetrate. Lying on her side, she slipped between two thick stools of cane stalks. Beyond that were more and still more.

She was covered with mud and sweat and blood and green stains from the weeds by the time she thought she'd gone deep enough to escape discovery. Then she had time to think, for the first time since she heard that terrible whack from the porch.

She was shaking, her teeth chattering, but she was also so hot she felt she might burst. There was no breeze—almost no air—down at the roots of the cane. Then she understood what shook her. Fury, not fear or cold, had set her to shivering.

She had lost, in those few moments, her entire family. She suffered no grief for her father—George's knife had saved him many weeks of suffering. But Sunny was young and healthy and full of life. Dumb, yes, but if that were a hanging offense almost everybody would be lined up at the gallows.

She gripped the wood handle of the knife, its wicked curve satisfying something deep inside her. Her mother used to rip open a hog's belly as easy as cutting butter with that thing. If she could get within reach—but George's arms were twice the length of hers. The cane knife added a good yard or so to that. She would never get close enough.

Something slithered behind her in the litter of dropped cane leaves. She went still, her shaking forgotten. A moccasin didn't have to get within arm's reach of anyone. He stayed down low, where your feet would step, and if you didn't watch you could step right onto one of the stinking creatures.

She closed her eyes and breathed deeply. She was educated, heir to the entire tradition of western culture. She need not panic, now that she was hidden. She had time to think and to plan, even if George did intend to kill the witness to his double murder.

She had read many things outside the normal course of study. She had read the works of Hawking, who was taking physics outside the realm of normal reality. Studies of the brain, she remembered, hinted at tremendous possibilities. And her own people knew that you could make things happen, if you willed it strongly enough and had the stomach for it.

Hibiscus smiled, feeling the muscles of her cheeks tense in a grimace. Even as she relaxed, she heard the noisy progress of someone in the cane field, crunching and rustling and stomping and cursing.

Moving smoothly over the cane roots and around the stools, she slithered to more open ground. Rustles in the weeds marked the moccasins fleeing her progress, but she paid them no heed. She rose to her full height with her head up and her shoulders back. The knife in her hand was almost invisible in the twilight.

She moved toward the source of the sounds, compelled by something outside herself, as well as a surge of will from within. Her brain throbbed in her skull, forming a vision that she was bringing into focus.

Her bare foot came down on a snake, and she felt the electric tension of the muscle rings as the serpent fled from beneath her weight. It didn't coil, and it didn't bite, for she was now the snake's sister.

George heard her movements. He paused and called, "Woman! You come out here and talk to me. I won't hurt you, but you better come out." He chuckled quietly, and she chuckled too, knowing that he thought he had deceived her.

Now it was almost dark. The palest glimmer of a moon rode above the western trees, giving just enough illumination to allow her to see his eyes glinting and his white teeth grinning amid the cane. "Why, here you come, Honey. That's a good gal. Right to me...yes, Ma'am!"

She felt his arm rise, saw in her inner vision the cane knife poised to slice through her. But she came more swiftly than he dreamed she would, and the hog knife slid under his ribcage. She jerked it up, just as she had seen her mother do so many times.

Something warm covered her hands. The cane-knife fell through the leaves, swishing down until it thudded into the damp soil. George stood stiff, his shape a blot of blackness against the darkness of the cane. Then he toppled, face down, amid the whispering leaves.

"George," she said softly. "George?"

There was, of course, no answer. She turned toward the house, wiping her sticky hands on her skirt. After a bit, she began, very quietly, to laugh.

As I said earlier, bird hunting is pretty popular here. So is revenge, particularly if it seems you might get away with it.

HALLIMORE'S DOG

I swear to God I didn't mean to do it. It happened so fast—the dogs flushed a covey of quail, I swung my twelve-gauge to follow them, and Clay Hallimore's big red face loomed up in my sights. It was so easy. So accidental!

The gun barked, and his face exploded into hamburger. I was as surprised and sick as if it had been completely an accident, one of those awful hunting mishaps that always happen to somebody else. My belly turned over, and I threw up right where I stood. The deputies found it later and it counted in my favor.

Clay's setter came running back, his little black eyes on me all the time. He was a fine retriever, and he'd been looking for shot birds, but you'd have thought he was a bloodhound the way he went for me. It was like he knew I'd finally got even with Clay....

I had to kill him, or he'd have killed me. He went down with a load of shot in his head, but he kept moving toward me, and it took two in the heart to stop him. Then I had to get rid of him before I called the sheriff. Shooting his master might seem like an accident, but there was no way to explain shooting the dog as well.

I caught him by ears and tail, to keep blood off me, and carried him down the draw into a dry wash, where I kicked dirt over him. Nobody was going to worry about a dog, with everything else going on.

When I went back to start putting on my act, that damn Hallimore was moving. You can shoot a man once, by accident, but twice has to be murder. I couldn't finish him off without putting my own tail in a crack. But the way his head was all torn up, I couldn't see him living long; if he did, surely he wouldn't be able to say anything.

So I went into my act, yelling for help, bending over him to beg him to be all right. It was too far for anyone to hear, of course, so I broke into a staggering run toward the store on the county road and screamed like a stepped-on cat. Old man Benedict called the sheriff, the doctor, and even the preacher. Then Mrs. Bonine, the store-keeper's wife, took me to their living quarters in the back of the store and made me lie down. By then I needed to. I'd convinced myself I'd lost my oldest friend, and I had a serious case of hysterics.

The county cars came skidding up before long, and I got up and went to show them where Clay was. Bonine and Mr. Benedict had gone on ahead, of course, to take care of Clay while the law got there, but the deputies were from the other side of the county and had to have a guide.

They treated me mighty tender, and once we got in sight of the mess they left me in the car while they went across the cornfield to the men hunkered down around Hallimore. After a while an ambu-lance screamed up, and I had myself a real good and genuine cry. First time in my life! That didn't hurt me a bit with the law, either.

Clay was in the operating room for hours, and they told his wife he wasn't going to make it. Then they said he might make it. Then, by God, he lived, but he couldn't see or hear or speak. Probably never would, they said.

Lizzie was a kindly woman, and she told my wife, "You tell Jock not to worry. He hasn't killed my Clay. Maybe that'll comfort him some. I know he's suffered something awful."

Well, I had, but not from what she thought. I was scared to death somebody would dig back into the past and remember the old tale about Clay and my Pa. Of course, nobody but me ever put eve-rything together and understood that Clay could have missed run-ning over Pa, even if it was dark, on a twisty road, and Pa was drunk as a boiled owl.

Still, a man lying in the middle of a sand road shows up as a dark patch, however dark the night may be. The Hallimores had itched for years over the fence-line that Pa disputed and won in court. I figured that Clay saw his chance and got even without risk-ing anything.

The same as I had done.

But nobody called to mind what happened twenty years ago, and nobody doubted that I was shattered over shooting a fellow I'd grown up neighbors with. After a few weeks I let myself get better, a bit at a time, and went back to work at my winter job at the John Deere place, mechanicking.

I'd got away with it, slick as a whistle.

Over the next six months, I decided something was wrong with my eyes. I kept seeing something, just off the edge of my vision. Then it began to come into focus. Damned if a dog wasn't following me when I walked across my own land. I'd put in a corn crop that spring, and it kept me busy thinning it. I was out a lot, and off to one side there was always a black dog, watching me. One morning, with white mist on the ground and the sun just coming up, I saw him plain, sitting in the ditch. I whistled at it. Lots of bird dogs get lost, but this one didn't come running.

When I got within six feet of it, I saw it was that setter of Hallimore's. The marks of my birdshot were all over his head and chest. He couldn't be there, but I aimed my twenty-two. Before I could pull the trigger, he was gone, popped like a bubble.

Damn!

From that day on I never took a step outside that I didn't hear the pad of paws in the trail behind me. Sometimes I saw him; most often there was nothing there, just those quiet sounds in the dust. It got to me. I made a pretty fair crop, and my boss in Dalby let me off for a week in the middle of September. Said I looked peaked and needed a rest.

I did, at that. We went to Galveston, stayed in a nice hotel, and laid around on the beach doing nothing much in particular. There was no black setter there, and I felt a lot better.

Quick as we got home, though, there he was again. I never hunted any more, just went out when I had to fix fence or tend the cattle or go to work. The dog came closer, clear up to the house. I could look out at night and there'd be two bright eyes shining and a row of white teeth. His black coat didn't show up against the dark.

Then it started talking to me. Not so my wife could hear, but in the night, real soft, after I went to sleep. It talked in Clay's voice that was as familiar to me as my own Pa's.

"Jock," it'd begin, "you just don't know how black it is. Nothing comes in. Nothing can get out. Silence and darkness, that's all. If it wasn't for old Whiz, I'd go teetotal crazy, but he's the best dog anybody ever had. He didn't go wherever dead dogs go to. He came to me. He's the only one can hear me or carry word for me."

I woke up in a cold sweat and looked out my window. Whiz was looking right back at me, through the glass. I scootched down and hid my face against Trudy's back, but that didn't stop the dog.

"You're the only one can see and hear us, Jock. Proves what a good friend you are. The only person in the world I can get through to. We're grateful you let us come visit you. It gets so lonesome here in the dark. We'll be your friends forever, Jock. You'll never have to worry about being lonely. We'll see to that."

STRANGE DOIN'S IN THE PINE HILLS, by Ardath Mayhar * 49

Didn't the fool know I shot him on purpose? But he sounded as if he meant every word. The dog knew—why couldn't he make his master understand I tried to murder him? But maybe the communication only went one way.

I tried talking, confessing, out in the woods while the dog padded along behind me. I went back to hunting, because there was no security inside the house any more, and I talked and talked while we trudged through the fields. Nothing helped. I had nothing but gratitude till it made me plumb sick.

I stood it for a year. When I couldn't take any more, I went and finished off Clay. Wasn't hard—I just crept into his hospital room one night and shut off his oxygen for a minute. Then I turned it back on, hid till the nurse went back around the corner, and left. They expected him to die anyway, and nobody was surprised.

It didn't help a bit. By then he and his damn dog were so used to trailing after me they didn't know how to quit.

Which is why I'm writing this letter. I want Trudy to know that I'm not killing myself because of anything she's done. She's been true blue all the way. I just can't live with my ghosts any more, and I want her to understand that.

I don't give a damn about anybody else.

Signed:

Jock Falls Wyndom

Political office holders in East Texas wrote the rule book on crook-edness. Doris's experience reflects those of others who have been framed to hide Good Old Boys' misdeeds.

FUNGUS GROWS IN THE DARK

It had been one of the worst of days, though most were hectic and stressful in Doris's job. The Commissioners had met twice in executive session, and nobody seemed to be able to find out what the object was. As usual, Doris thought, they were meeting illegally to cover up some more of their petty misdeeds, but she didn't worry about it. It was hard enough to adhere to the complex and contradictory orders that came down to her from week to week.

Everyone in the office was on edge, for the bunch of Good Old Boys who ran the county could turn nasty if anyone questioned them or resisted their pet projects. Such a project was being opposed, right now, by a citizens' group, and the County Judge was livid.

But Doris covered her computer terminal, rechecked the records for the cash turned over to the Treasurer, and made certain that her books were in order. That was automatic, for back in Beaumont she had been the treasurer herself, and she knew how to keep accurate records and to make sure everything was ready to audit at any time. Indeed, she'd kept proof of all the instructions she'd been given, because they were just too flaky to let them pass.

Here there was seldom an outside audit, and when it came, everyone knew long in advance. She wondered why they bothered. The orders they gave her sounded fishy most of the time, and she wondered what became of some of the funds transferred so frequently between departments.

She made sure the other women were out of the office before clicking off the light. Her heels tapped loudly on the marble floor as she moved down the corridor toward the stair. Usually the last to leave, except for custodians and the sheriff's department on the first floor of the courthouse, she was glad of the quiet time before getting home to her husband and daughters.

Her car sat at the far end of the lot. As she approached it, the sound of footsteps alerted her. There had been muggings, even here under the sheriff's elbow, so to speak, and she didn't intend to add to their number. But as the man stepped beneath the light post she saw that it was Pepper, one of the deputies.

"You startled me," she said. "Good night."

He cleared his throat, and something about the way he sounded brought her up short. "Clem, are you all right?" she asked.

"I'm sorry, Miz Rogers. I've got to do this. Sheriff told me to. I hope you understand...." He paused and looked down at her, his entire body expressing extreme discomfort.

"I got a warrant for your arrest."

The words flowed past her, meaningless. Impossible.

Then she felt a jolt, as if someone had hit her in the stomach. Suddenly, she saw a pattern in the long history of conflicting, senseless orders that had come down the chain of command from those running the county. She swallowed hard. At last she managed to say, "And what is the charge, Clem?"

He squirmed visibly in the harsh, blue-white light of the standard. "Embezzlement."

She knew that before he spoke. They had set her up and thought she had gone like a woolly lamb to slaughter. Used to controls and cross-checks, she had never quite believed that someone was siphoning off tax and fee moneys. Now it was perfectly clear, and she cursed herself for ten kinds of a fool for failing to see it sooner.

She'd been warned about going to work for the county, after she and Bob moved here. Now she understood why. She thanked God for the warning. "So what now?" she asked. It wasn't Clem's fault, and he obviously hated what he was doing. There was no need to make him more uncomfortable.

"Got to take you in and book you, Ma'am."

"I get a phone call, right? My husband is at home with the kids, expecting me in about ten minutes." She wanted to scream, to hit him with her handbag or her shoe and run off into the darkness, but she knew she had to keep control, to be calm and cool and unperturbed. If she managed to do that, perhaps someone might let something slip.

"You can do that in the office, Ma'am. I'm real sorry."

He sounded sorry, too. Poor kid—his uncle was Commissioner for Precinct Six, and slipped relatives into county jobs as if it were legal.

Doris turned, her head high, anger filling her with determination. They were going to have to fight for this one. She wouldn't go down tamely like Jenny Turner in the County Auditor's office, framed and convicted without protest. This time those bastards were going to feel pain, no matter how it turned out.

The combination police station and sheriff's office took up the bottom floor of the ancient brick structure housing the Amberson County courthouse. The hallway, painted a sick green, was lit by forty-watt bulbs, which left shadows lurking in odd corners, but she felt no unease. Once she was in a cell she might begin to cry, but for now Doris Rogers was furious.

* * * * * * *

She got her call at the phone booth, using her own coin. Kenneth was dumbfounded when she told him, and then he was furious too. But Doris had now had time to cool off a bit and get her wits together.

"Don't call a lawyer yet. Let me spend the night in jail," she murmured into the phone, glancing aside at the deputy, who pretended not to be trying to hear what she said. "That will make a wrongful arrest and imprisonment suit just that much better. And remember where I hid my files and tapes. Thank God I didn't try hiding them in the house—don't let on that you know anything about them though."

She breathed the last words, hoping he would hear. Clem must not catch them.

Actually, it was unlikely that anyone would suspect her of keeping her own account of the strange orders she was given. No other woman working here had ever been able to defend herself against unjust accusations. The Good Old Boys had gotten away with this sort of thing for so long, it probably never occurred to them that an end might come.

A woman jailer she knew slightly from church strip-searched her and took her wristwatch, handbag, and glasses. Doris felt that Susan was as embarrassed as she was, trying hard not to show it. When that was done, Susan handed her the overall in bright orange and led her to a cell.

"They'll likely make your picture and fingerprint you and all that tomorrow," she said. "Most of 'em's gone to the football game tonight."

Just about everyone else had too, Doris decided. The small jail was empty except for a couple of jailers, after Susan's shift ended and she left. There was the distant clank of a mop-bucket; Doris felt sure someone was cleaning up, but she couldn't see a soul from her back-tier cell.

The lights dimmed, though they were still too bright for sleeping. She stretched herself on the hard cot and stared at the sick-green ceiling. A roach big enough to pull a plow crawled across as she watched and slipped into a crack in the plaster.

Doris shuddered. Never had she dreamed, even in a nightmare, that she would be in such a position!

Something woke her, much later. A thud—that would be the heavy door into the office section closing. Steps approached along the narrow corridor. She pretended to be asleep, some atavistic instinct warning her to see who was coming before she responded.

Square shoulders, bullet head—it was the sheriff himself! Damn! She was almost sure he was in with the power brokers that ran the city, the county, and the world, as far as local citizens were concerned.

Something clanged loudly against the bars. "You! Get up and come over here!"

She opened her eyes and gave her coldest stare. "I do not obey your orders," she said. "If you have something to say, spit it out. If not, go away and allow me to sleep." She deliberately used her most fastidious "city girl" accent.

His thick neck turned red. The lock creaked, and he pushed the door wide.

Doris was on her feet instantly, getting ready for anything he might try. She hadn't lived most of her life in Los Angeles for nothing. Her father had insisted that she learn basic self-defense, and though the sheriff was too big and too powerful for her to defeat, he'd know he'd been in a fight.

But he didn't bother with anything fancy. Those long, brawny arms reached for her, and the cell was too small to avoid them. A fist came at her. She ducked too slowly. Stars burst inside her skull, and she dropped like a stone into darkness.

* * * * * * *

Doris felt herself floating upward, her arms spread, her legs lower than her chest. She caught her breath, choked, and flailed desperately, trying to reach the top of the water. Sputtering, she surfaced and tried to kick toward the overgrown bank some yards away.

The pain in her legs was agonizing, and she sank again. But she had caught one valuable breath, and she moved her arms, making it up once more. This time she knew not to move her legs. That would kill her, without any doubt. Instead she kept breathing the way she'd been taught as a child at the local pool.

With her hands, she moved herself through the murky water toward the reeds lining the shore. What she'd do when she arrived was a question to be answered later.

It took a long time. As she struggled forward, keeping those shattered legs as quiet as possible, she began to recall what had happened. But there was one glaring gap—what had Sheriff Allen done to her? And how had he thought he'd get away with throwing her into a river?

Her outstretched fingers touched slimy reeds. She struggled forward, and this time she caught a handful of the stuff and pulled herself into the thick growth. Her knee bumped mud; she was now close enough to climb out—if, of course, her legs had been in working order.

Doris braced herself with both hands, staring up the gentle slope of wet grass and muck. It should be so easy to get up there, clear of the water, the snakes (she'd been told horror stories about water moccasins), the possible—she shivered—alligators that lived in the waters of East Texas.

Spurred by the thought, she pulled herself against the slope and lay on her stomach. She moved one knee, just a bit, and the resulting agony told her that was not going to work. Doris took a deep breath, feeling water flutter in her throat and lungs. She still had elbows, by God!

Digging into the soft ground, she dragged herself forward, one elbow at a time, until she was almost out of the stream. Her heart was running away, her chest hurting, her head feeling as if it might explode. *What must my blood pressure be?* she wondered.

Resting for a moment, she listened hard. Above the flip of willow leaves in the breeze and the croaking of a million frogs, she could hear a rumble that had to be trucks on a highway. Not close, no. But it couldn't be that far.

Already her elbows felt raw, but she gritted her teeth and moved again up the slope, a few inches at a time. When she lay flat again, she was on level ground in a patch of sunlight. Her clammy orange coverall stuck to her skin and now felt steamy instead of chilly. But she'd be hotter before she was through.

Beyond the flattish ridge edging the small river there was a thick stand of willows. She'd never be able to crawl through there, and it would be a fine place to find snakes as well. The ridge seemed to follow the river faithfully, and if she crept along it, dragging her useless legs behind her, eventually she would die or reach help.

Doris dropped her head on her arms, tears leaking from her eyes. Damn! Damn! Damn! She'd never done anything in her life to deserve something like this.

She sniffed hard and raised her head. Neither had any of those women who were now on parole or serving jail terms for things they hadn't done. She wondered why, of them all, the county had decided that she posed a threat—had Clem heard what she told Ken, after all?

But that was impossible. She had hardly spoken loudly enough for Ken to hear her. And Clem, she was almost sure, didn't like what was being done to her. She'd noticed that he was off duty before she finished being processed.

Had anyone suspected that she was keeping tapes of the orders she'd been given? That voice-activated mini-recorder in her purse was too small to show, and it didn't make any noise. Her photocopies of the memos had been made after hours on her own paper. Nobody had been around except the janitors, and they hadn't even been on the same floor at the time.

How and why? As she plowed along, her elbows skinless and bleeding, she worried at the questions. That kept her from thinking about all the varied miseries in her battered body.

At least the legs had gone numb. If she had a spinal injury, it must be below the waist. The thought of being a cripple the rest of her life didn't disturb her much...not yet. Once she reached help, she was going to blow those bastards out of the water.

Allen, of course, would be the first and worst. Then Eva Janks, the county judge, realtor, and general wheeler-dealer. Oscar Revell was too dumb to understand much of anything, but he was as crooked as he could manage to be.

The other commissioners were yes-men, rubber stamps for the machinations of the others. They deserved to suffer for having no spines or brains. Thinking about what she would do to them made the next hundred yards easier than it might have been.

The sun moved across and began its downward slide. The shade of the willows kept the worst of the sun off her, but by then she was exhausted, scraped, battered, and bruised from head to foot. The orange coverall was worn away to shreds beneath her dragging stomach and legs, letting the patches of gravel along the way attack skin that had been somewhat protected by the uniform.

It grew dark. Doris rested under a clump of button willow bushes, feeling that she had done all she could do. Now she would either bleed to death from the many shallow scratches or possible internal injuries, or she wouldn't. Her children would never know what happened to her; Ken would be wild with worry. She would be dead and out of it, but what if the county government tried to go after her family?

It was like a shot of adrenaline. She was not going to allow that. Again she elbowed forward, dragging her painful body, her mind wandering in a fog of fever. Everything else seemed to stop while she pushed her failing body onward, her will the only part of her that still held to its purpose.

* * * * * * *

Doris woke, sputtering. A large wet tongue was licking her cheek, saliva trickling down over her nose and lips. The damp soil was cold under her face, and she turned away from the helpful dog to find that it was daylight again.

She tried to push herself up, to dig in with her elbows, but her arms had stiffened in the night and she could no longer move them. She felt frozen to the ground, only her head able to move on her neck. She drew a shuddering breath. To die on a riverbank attended by a friendly dog was a better fate than lying in the muck of the stream bed to be eaten by crawfish, she thought.

A whistle shrilled. She moaned faintly, unable to make enough noise to catch anyone's attention. The dog, however, knew what must be done. He gave a last sloppy lick at her hair, and she heard his paws padding away up the ridge.

"My God!" That was a voice she knew. Dennis Wheeler ran a dairy near the river someplace, she knew. It must be nearby.

She felt hands touch her hesitantly. She had to look like death warmed over, she thought, as he turned her carefully on her side. Her eyes seemed bleared, but she made out the ruddy face, now creased with concern.

"What the hell happened to you?" he asked. Then with a quick indrawing of breath he recognized her. "Doris? Doris Rogers?"

She grunted softly. Having gone all the way through pain and out the other side, now she was numb, unable to move anything. But her will was still there, if nothing else. "Sher'f," she moaned.

"I'll get him soon as we take you in to the house. Don't worry!"

"No!" That came out clearly, sharp on the dawn air. "He...put...me...river."

Wheeler stared down, trying to understand. Then his eyes widened. "He done this to you? The Sheriff? My God!" He turned to the dog. "You go fetch Mama, Harold. Fetch Mama, you hear?"

The German shepherd looked up at his master, wagged his tail, and took off again up the ridge. Wheeler went down the bank carefully, wet his handkerchief, and came back to dab at Doris's mud and blood-smeared face. She could see how terrible she must look reflected in his expression, but it was all she could do to keep breathing. Reassuring her rescuer was beyond her.

Someone came at last, but by then she was all but out of it. When they lifted her onto a stretcher and moved her, she passed out, but she came to as they slipped her into an ambulance. "Not to Amberson Hospital. Go to Laf...." she coughed harshly, feeling water still sloshing in her lungs. "Go to Lafferty General. Call husband." She felt her eyes closing, but she managed to gasp, "718-6767."

The moves after that were dim intervals of agony interspersed with long patches of unconsciousness. When she woke fully, after a long time, she was lying on her back, her legs pulled up onto a framework and secured there. Her arms wouldn't move at first, though at last she managed to wiggle the fingers of her right hand.

Her skin burned and stung. Her legs ached violently, and her head felt as if some demonic imp was using it as an anvil. Every time her heart beat, surges of red and orange lit the insides of her eyelids. That wouldn't do—she opened her eyes.

Ken was there in the recliner beside the bed. As she focused on him, he realized that she was awake. His familiar face bent close, though he understood, evidently, that nothing must touch her for a very long time.

"Hey, kid," he said, his voice gruff. "You had me worried there for a while."

She licked her lips, and he got a glass from the tray and held it for her to sip water. That helped, and she managed to ask, "'M I unner arrest?"

His face went grim. "They tried, goddamn 'em. No sooner did the Amberson bunch find out where you are than they sent a deputy with a warrant. But I got your stuff out of the hollow stump in our woods and took it to the DA over here in Lafferty County yesterday morning—you've been out for two days, by the way.

"He got the interim judge of the Second District Court to issue an injunction protecting you from harassment by anyone, official or not, until he can get the attorney general's office to look into this."

He grinned down at her, and for a moment she felt nothing but triumph. "You got 'em, baby. Cold as dead catfish. Once they listened to those tapes you made over the last months, they got on the stick. They've been waiting like vultures circling a dying cow for years to catch those jokers, but nobody has ever had the goods on them before."

Doris sighed and closed her eyes. Then she opened them again. "It was Sheriff Allen who came into the cell and knocked me out. I'm not certain he was the one who broke my legs and threw me in the river."

Her husband looked more dangerous than she had ever seen him in all their years together. "He ran over you with his own car. Twice. His treads are marked on your thighs as plain as paint, and they've been photographed. You were just lucky that he missed your upper body and your head.

"Whoever put you in the water did it under his orders, it's certain. He's going to the wall with his cronies, Dodo. You won't have to testify at all, unless you want to."

She sneezed suddenly, and every nerve stood up and screamed. Once she eased a bit, her old anger came back, sending warmth through her.

"Oh, I'll testify, Ken. You'd better bet I'll testify. Can you see me, all black and blue and wrapped in bandages like a mummy, being wheeled up to the witness box and telling what happened to me? With all that stuff as evidence?" She sniffed and tried to smile. "I want to see them suffer."

He reached out gently to touch her forehead with one finger. "We'll see to that," he said.

* * * * * * *

The day she wheeled herself into the courtroom, bandages still necessary for the worst of the cuts, and bruises still washes of pale yellow and green on her arms and face, she could, if she insisted, have walked with two canes. Yet Doris wanted to show to the fullest effect the thing that man had done.

She saw understanding in the eyes of the ex sheriff, and when the jury returned its verdict they, too, had gotten the message. With her documentation and her own story, they put him away for a long time, even in these days of ineffective sentences.

I have always thought of this part of the country as a sort of cultural Black Hole. There are strange survivals from the past—habits and rituals and almost Neanderthal attitudes. We have our share of really crazy people, too—more than it is comfortable to think about.

KING OF THE SLOUGH

The gill net grew like magic. The shuttle flipped in and out, back and forth in the gnarled fingers, and King Deport never looked down to see what they were doing. He had made so many over the years that those fingers needed no supervision from the rest of King. Which was fine with me—that left time and attention for storytelling.

Make no mistake, King's stories were the best of their kind. I'd thought it when I was a bug-eyed boy of eleven, and when I went back as a grown man, I found them even better than I remembered, a funny reversal of the usual order of things. I might not have gone back to the woodsy East Texas country where I grew up, if it hadn't been for King and his tales. My folks were gone, moved to Houston, and I hadn't much to return to but the woods and the river and King.

He was the one who started me collecting tall tales and strange stories, first for fun and then for profit. Once I had my degrees, it was a part-time profession, then full-time. The first book-length collection hit the market just as people were ripe for nostalgia mixed with humor. As it was the result of years of research, it also hit the academics favorably. That first book made a hefty profit for the publisher, and they wanted more.

I had some fine years of travel to Europe, Africa, the Orient, even Lapland and Alaska, seeking out oldsters with tales to tell. And the books did well enough to free me from teaching and the apple-polishing that goes along with it. That suited me fine.

Once I had enough squirreled away to take care of myself and my wife for the rest of our lives, I just sat back and asked myself what it was that I wanted to do. At forty I wasn't ready to quit work, certainly. The children were young, but they were also independent and busy. Callie, my wife, had her anthropological research to do, and didn't want to worry about my being at loose ends.

That's when I decided to go back to the root and source of my interests, back to Skillet Bend and the river, the big woods that even the loggers hadn't been able to clear out—and King Deport. He was still active and alert, though he was at least eighty. He had seemed old when I was eleven, which meant he was probably forty then. You can hardly produce wrinkles as deep as his in less time than that.

I packed up my kit, kissed Callie goodbye, waved to the boys, who were headed out on an expedition of their own, and took off for Skillet Bend, Texas, population 225. My Dad's old friend, the post-master, had volunteered to put me up, when I wrote to ask about King, so I had a headquarters right down close to the river and the river bottom for which I was headed.

I was shocked when I saw the way the woods had been devastated, as I drove through the cut-over remnants toward the town. The primal forest of my boyhood was reduced to scrub and stands of pole pine that the timber companies planted where old forests of mixed hickory and gum and oak and pine and ash had stood. I didn't like it, and I wondered about the wildlife. I figured King could tell me. He watched the wild with care, and he always had a sensible view of anything going on.

Not being eleven any more, I minded my manners and went to dinner with some old friends of my folks. Then I went fishing over the weekend with Ben. So it was three days before I could take off on my own and scout out the woodsy world that had been the joy of my boyhood. Once I got right deep into the wild country, it wasn't so bad—there were still places so remote and swampy that it was too hard to get in with loaders and skidders and trucks.

Down on the river was state land. They had built a big lake twenty years ago and bought up all the access land upstream from the place where the Nichayac ran into the catchment. There was still some huge timber there, far back in where timber thieves couldn't handily go. I hoped the cutting on the banks had been done by thieves. I still had the illusion that the state had more sense than to cut off ground-cover along the waterside.

At the mud ramp, where fishermen launched their boats, I backed my borrowed pickup truck and off-loaded the light aluminum boat I had also borrowed. To get in to find King, you had to know how to do it. I hoped I remembered.

Once I was sliding down the current between the overhanging

willows lining the bank, I felt suddenly as if the decades had evaporated. I was still a boy on the way to see my friend and hero. I almost checked out my old trotline spots, out of habit, as I moved along, but the dead trees I'd used as markers were long gone, and the willows there were the great-grandchildren of those to which I had tied my lines.

So I eased along, using the paddle now and again to maneuver around a sand bar or a snag. Before I knew it, I was at the mouth of the creek where I had to leave the boat. There was a good stout post there, where King's infrequent visitors could tie up securely. His own boat was hidden someplace so secure that not even I had ever been able to find it.

Once afoot, I went along the worn path, smelling the mellow woods-scent of home. There wasn't another to match it. Africa smelled strong and alien. Europe had a distant effluvium of too many people in the same place for too long. The Orient mostly stunk. East Texas woods smelled like rain on new grass, leaves quietly mulching for generations, and strong old trees waiting out the years wrapped in clean and peeling bark.

I was grinning like a fool by the time I rounded the last bend in the path and saw King's shanty leaning against the tremendous pine he'd chosen as its prop and stay. I paused and pursed up my lips. The tooo-whee! whistle that had been our signal cut through the rustling quiet.

There was no reply for maybe a minute and a half. Then a tremulous reply came to my ears. I ran to the door and pushed. It hung low on its leather hinges and scraped the floor, but I automatically lifted, and there was King, sitting by a smudge of fire, though it was already getting hot so late in the spring. His lap was full of gillnet, as usual, though two hoop-nets leaned against the far wall, one already fitted with all its netting, the other halfway done.

He looked up but didn't try to rise. That told me a lot about what time had done to him. In the old days, he would have met me before I got to the door.

"Bam," he murmured. "Alabama Vincent Tremaine! Never thought to see you agin, boy. Come set by me and tell me how it's gone, all these years since your folks moved off. By gum, boy, I never would of dreamed you'd come back. They tell me you teach in a college, or did. And write books!" His tone was full of awe, and I suddenly recalled that he never went to school in his life. He couldn't read a book, much less write one.

I sat beside him on the short-legged stool that had always been my place, and told him about my life and travels. His questions and comments amazed me with their insight into the ways people related with each other, no matter where they were. When I said something about it, he laughed.

"Folks is folks, Bam, wherever they live. All of 'em pretty well act the same when you poke 'em with a stick. "

Which I suspect may be perfectly true.

Then I questioned him about the woods and the beasts he knew so well. I also asked about the depredations of the loggers, and that was when his face went grim, his fingers slowed on the shuttle.

"Stupid bastards! Log the riverbanks so the land just slides off down into the Gulf of Mexico. Cut the woods and leave the critters to move or die. They'd be right down here with their damn chainsaws and mechanical monsters, if...." His voice dwindled to silence.

"If what?" I asked. There had been something in his tone that sent a chill up my back.

He looked at me through the light, which was partly sunlight filtered through that granddaddy pine tree, partly red light from the coals on his hearth. His eyes, black as swamp water, were thoughtful, sizing me up as a man, the way they'd done when I was a boy. He nodded, a mere dip of the chin.

"I reckon I can tell you, Bam. Nobody else knows, but you I can trust. Could from Day One. Only been two boys I ever knowed that was trusty, and t'other was my son. He's been gone...but that's of no account. You I can trust, same as I could him. But never let a hint slip, not till I'm dead and gone."

"Hope to die," I said, with the old fervor.

He sighed. His hands moved faster, as the gillnet grew. "Well, you know I heired all this land from my folks. My great-great-great-granddaddy had it on a grant from the King of Spain. That's why all the oldest sons was named King, kind of in appreciation, you see?" I nodded, for I'd heard that before. "I never let no logger set foot here and never will as long as I hold breath. They know that. Many's the lawyer's come all the way, duded up in shiny boots and fancy khakis, to see can they hornswoggle me into signing some of their papers."

He cocked his head to look me in the eye. "Happen you remember I can't read. Don't sign nothing I can't read, so I don't sign nothing at all. I send 'em all back to town to Mr. Jenkins. He taken care of my Dad, and he's took care of me. But I guess some of them bastards figured I was getting too old to look to my affairs. You know better, boy, and others do too, but loggers ain't what you'd call real bright, or they'd be doing something else in the world besides messing up the woods."

"They tried to steal your timber?" I asked. The idea shocked me, though I knew timber theft was common.

"You recall Rupe Hendricks?" he asked.

The name rang a dim bell in my memory. A shape formed around the name: a tough, square boy with just enough brains not to be an idiot, but not any over and to spare. He had, if I recalled, enough meanness to make up for any amount of dumbness. "I remember," I said.

"Thought you might. You beaten the tar out of him once, when he made trouble for your little brother. Well, he come down here onto my land, marking my trees. They figured that if they knowed just what they wanted to take out, then they could sneak in, cut 'em, and float 'em downriver, catching 'em at the bend above Bobcat Creek. I dunno how they thought to get the things to water, but they might have intended to bring mules across my property line to drag 'em. Anyway, they sent Rupe in to mark."

He bent and lifted a snuff can from the hearth and spat a stream of tobacco juice into it, put the lid on neatly, and set it back. "That boy knowed timber, if nothing else. He marked the big walnut by the creek, first off. All the biggest pines. Must've hurt his soul to pass by mine here, but he didn't dare come close to the house. There's a big stand of ash he intended to take—every bit of it, but I dunno what for.

"All the big hickories was marked, probably for railroad ties. He didn't miss a trick. But of course I caught on the first time I cast around the woods. You can't mark a tree so I don't see it. I didn't know who, right then, but I for certain knowed what." He leaned back in his hickory splint chair to ease his back and stretched his fingers, cracking the knotted joints. Then he picked up the shuttle.

"You recall the big slough over at the edge of my land, where Grampa Catfish lives?"

Having tried for half my young life to catch Grampa, I would never forget that muddy stretch that was so much deeper than it looked.

"That's where I caught up with him. Waited for days before he come, but I knowed he would. That stand of pine has been what most of the lawyers wanted, and I knowed no timber-marker could pass it up. Soon's as I seen it was Rupe, I knowed I was in trouble. You know how mean he was, and I was pretty old and stove up, even then. In my prime, I'd have tied him into a bow-knot and hung him in a tree, but that's a good many years back, and was then too.

"Anyway, he looked up from his mark and seen me watching. Never paused nor howdied, just come at me like a catamount. Now you know, Bam, I never go no place without my stick. Even when I was young, I taken it along for snakes. You can't carry a stick for sixty years without getting to know how to handle it. So I knocked him in the head, hard as I could. Didn't faze him." He chuckled.

"Onliest thing that boy ever used his head for was to hold up his hat. Solid bone, it was. I tripped him, next pass he made at me, and set on his back while I got my wind. Had to keep whacking his head to keep him from bucking me off, but it worked."

I felt a cold knot in my stomach. If what I was thinking had happened....

"Then I got mad. Here was this peckerwood cruising my land, ready to steal my trees, and trying to beat me up for catching him at it. Purely unreasonable, I thought it to be. I seldom lose my temper, Bam. One reason I live so far from folks is because I know I've got one, so I keep it where it can't do no harm. But he come to me. And I was hot. Hot as a firecracker."

"What did you do...with him?" I asked, half choked.

"Why I fed him to Grampa Catfish. Drug him kicking and squealing right to the edge of the slough, after I'd tied him up with my belt and his galluses. Called the Old Man offen the bottom. Did you know I could do that? We come to an agreement, long years ago, boy. I'd go down and feed him trash fish outen my nets. He knowed when I called it meant food. Anyway, I called him and shoved Rupe in.

"In a minute, there come a thrashing in the water. Grampa must weigh a couple of hundred pounds by now. Thereabouts. There was some bubbles and a bit of blood, and then nothing. So I come home and thought about it." He stopped his busy fingers and looked at me.

"You see, boy, when you're old as I am, used to living alone in the woods, you can't stand trials and jails and all such like that. Even did they find me innocent of anything but self defense, I'd die in the middle of it. I've got to live out my time right here, taking care of my woods. So I never said nothing. And if the thieves suspicioned what happened, they kept it to themselves. Couldn't do much else, could they?

"Rupe's little wife is married to a real man, now. Got two little girls and is happier than she's ever been, I'm told. So I think what I done was maybe right. Not legal, but right."

I'd lived for a long time in the civilized world and been contaminated by its ways. Now I put myself back into the old ways I'd learned as a boy from the old men sitting in the store on Saturdays. You took care of yourself and your own. You asked nothing of anyone. You did what seemed right at the time and lived with the result.

By his own code, King had done nothing wrong.

I smiled. "I remember Rupe," I said. "If you hadn't killed him, he would have killed you, just for the hell of it. He tried it with me once, and he nearly succeeded. I figure Grampa Catfish was just what he deserved."

The rest of the visit was full of stories. Trees and animals I had known were dead but not forgotten. Places were changed, but King was not. When I left, he looked at me a bit anxiously.

"Hope to die," I repeated, and that was enough for him.

I have kept my word. Now he is dead and gone, his place tied up tightly as a gift to the Nature Conservancy, and I can tell his last, best tale. It's one that moderns won't approve, but that's neither here nor there. A day will come again, I suspect, when everyone must care for his own. King knew how. His generation knew how.

I am not so certain about ours.

Can you remember when the world was populated by mostly knee-caps and shoes? When everyone was bigger and taller and stronger than you, and you were at the mercy of nature? It isn't easy being a child, particularly when you have to deal with vicious adults....

RUNNER

The sharp scent of his mother's blood filled the boy's nostrils. He seemed to taste it on the back of his tongue, and it made him want to gag. Tam gulped, trying to hold his breath, to quiet his heartbeat. His stepfather had quick hearing; that racing heart might betray him to Mark, which would mean his own death.

Mom had seemed fond of Mark for a while, and she'd tried to make Tam like him too. Yet something about those frozen blue eyes had been terrifying. When Mark started beating Mom, Tam tried to get her to run away, but she refused.

"It's my house," Ruth Sechrist said. "He's spending my money, living on my inheritance. If we go, he'll get everything, and we'll have to hide and starve, because he'll kill us if he catches us. I've never been a runner. "Then she'd looked thoughtful. "But you have to run, Tam, if anything happens to me."

Now Tam remembered, listening to Mark search the house. Mark knew Tam had seen him hiding Mama's body, the boy felt sure. He knew Tam would tell what he knew, if he ever got the chance. Mark had to find him and kill him, if he could.

Tam grinned fiercely. Mark hadn't lived his life in this old house, creeping about the attics, finding the ducts installed when the house got its central heating. He probably didn't even know there were boy-sized ducts above the vent grillwork.

The boy sighed very gently and put his head on his knees, feeling the metal cold at his back. He was in his own grandfather's house, in a place to which Mark had never come. Only when he had given up his search could Tam hope to creep out and run.

Where? Grampa was long dead. There were cousins Mom had

mentioned once, but the boy had only a vague idea of where they lived. He couldn't guess whether they would welcome him or turn him away. Everyone knew Mark was his stepfather. Nobody knew that Mark was a murderer. He might be turned over to his Mom's killer, even by kin.

Shivering, the boy waited, while time crept past and the distant footsteps came closer. The murderer searched the big old house, one room at a time, taking care to lock each door behind him. Tam was surprised, as he heard the distant clunks of the old locks, that there were keys to those doors.

How could he hear those steps, so far away, through the solid wood of the house? Tam felt the subtle vibrations as Mark searched Mom's room, the linen closet, the guest bedroom, the nursery, the closet beside the stair.

The vent through which Tam had climbed opened above the top landing; he'd reached it by crawling up the carvings on the tall chest that stood there. Had his efforts left any betraying scuffs?

As Mark reached the top step, Tam held his breath, gripped his hands around his knees, and thought himself into another time and place, as Mom taught him to do long ago. If he was not here, then Mark could not possibly find him. He withdrew into the past, into another house where his Papa's mother had lived, with a deck extending over a river; he sat there, dangling his feet, looking down into the tan-green water, where minnows flirted.

One part of him kept track of Mark; the rest, the important part, relived that summer afternoon. When no sound, no vibration, no shift of the air spoke of another human presence, Tam allowed himself to drift back into his body. Even then he didn't venture to disturb the silence.

Mark might lie in wait in the house or the garden. Tam had no intention of falling into his hands. Mom had, in the past weeks, whispered to him when she came to tell him his bedtime story. Instead of the familiar tales, she began telling him how to protect himself. Neither of them mentioned Mark, but Tam knew.

Mom spoke of hiding places in the house and mentioned the old fire-rope that led from the upstairs dressing closet to the ground. She reminded him of things he had forgotten.

Now Tam wondered about the fire-rope. Did Mark know that the large, box-crammed closet even had a window, hidden behind all the rubbish it held? Or that it opened onto a long slope of roof? Below, the privet hedge grew close to the wall. There was good cover, if he could reach it.

Now the boy listened, holding his breath and trying to still the thudding of his heart. He heard the faint swish of wind over the shingled roof and the nervous skitter of mouse-claws in the attic beyond the duct.

Nobody was going to save him. Mom had kept repeating that. "You have to save yourself, Tam. He won't let me phone or go to town, so I can't get help. You have to get clean away and never look back."

Now he stretched cautiously, trying to get the circulation going in his cramped legs and arms. His back was stiff as he flattened himself along the metal tunnel, still silent, still careful, and wriggled toward the vent in the bedroom nearest the closet. He would have to go out into the hall. If Mark waited, hidden.... Tam shuddered.

He reached the dead end of the duct and paused for a long time, listening. The room below was dark: it was impossible to see through the grill over the vent. If Mark was waiting there, he had to breathe, maybe to cough or fidget. There was no sound at all. Even the wind had died.

Tam slithered to the edge of the vent again and peered down into the gloom below. Nothing. He reached down and twisted the catch, which gave with a sharp click. Startled, he paused to catch his breath before easing himself down into the box-like opening of the vent.

There was no tall furniture below; he would have to drop nine feet to the thick carpet. He just hoped the thump of his arrival wouldn't alert Mark. He held onto the bracket holding the grill in place, let himself down the length of his arms, and dropped to the floor. His knees took up the shock, and his sneakered feet made almost no sound, though a pall of dust rose from the carpet.

He held his nose, stifling a sneeze.

Again he waited, listening for any sound in the hall, but only a fresh gust of wind moaned around the old house. Tam crept across the floor on hands and knees. Lying flat, he peered under the loosely hung panel and saw a dim strip of the upstairs hall. Nobody there—not visible, anyway. The closet door creaked faintly as he opened it and again as he pushed it shut. Boxes were stacked from floor to ceiling, leaving only a crooked aisle for getting around. He moved between the musty ranks, smelling mothballs, old woolens, ancient paper, until he reached the window, which was covered by a torn green shade.

The rope was coiled around a stout hook let into the window facing. The window itself seemed to be stuck. It must have been years since anyone opened it, and Tam strained until his back hurt. At last the thing moved with a doleful screech, and he pushed it halfway up before it stuck again.

His heart galloping, Tam flung the coil of rope out and crawled out of the narrow opening. As he grasped the rope firmly and began to descend, the door of the closet crashed open and something ran headlong into the boxes, sending them tumbling—Mark, of course, but now it would take him a moment to get to the window.

Tam went down the sloping roof and into the hedge so fast that he burned his hands. Once amid the tangle of privet, he found the gap made by stray dogs and dived to the other side. Then he ran toward the old cool-room built into the stone bank of the creek. That was where he had watched Mark take Mama, and he knew he had to have evidence.

A shout of fury split the chill of early twilight, as Tam reached the steps and pushed open the thick door. Mama lay on the stone slab where pails of milk used to stand while the cream rose. He went to her side and touched her cheek. Cold. Very cold.

Her blouse was splotched with blood; that familiar scent almost made him retch. He tore off a generous patch of cloth, complete with stab-wound and blood, and moved up the steps to reconnoiter. Nobody was in sight, but he could hear footfalls pounding down the stair inside the house. He had to move.

The lane behind the barn led to Mr. Christie's cow barn. It was overgrown and rough, except for the narrow path, but Tam almost flew along it. As he ran he heard cursing far behind. Mark must have checked Mama's body and found the piece of blouse missing. The sound sent him faster along the track, to round the barn and speed up the drive toward the county road.

Then he skidded to a stop. Mark would surely take the car and search all the way to town. It was five miles to walk, and he was already pretty winded. He looked at the Christie house, where one dim light burned in the kitchen window. Mr. Christie didn't like Granddad, and he'd extended his dislike to the rest of the family. Tam had never spoken to him in his life. But he was a man, and a big one, if rather old. Surely he would care that Mama had been murdered.

Dragging his weary feet, the boy approached the kitchen and rapped timidly on the door. There came the scrape of a chair and the sound of steps on uncarpeted wood. The door opened and Christie's long face peered out. "Yes? Who's there?" It took a moment before he glanced down. Tam was now shivering and almost incapable of speech.

"Come in, boy. Come in and sit down and tell me why you're breakin' down my door so late." He gestured toward the kitchen, and Tam crept inside and dropped into a chair.

"I...I...," he gasped. Then, unable to speak, he held out the blood-soaked cloth he had carried so far.

"My God, boy, what you got there?" Christie took the strip in his big, calloused hands and stared down. Then he turned on another light, this one much brighter than the first, and stared at it again.

"Mama's...dead. Mark...killed her," Tam managed to say at last. "He'd kill me too, if he could...catch me." His heart was settling down, and his breath was coming more easily.

Christie looked up. "You're Gamble Forbes's grandson?"

Tam sighed. "Yessir. Mama's—was—his daughter."

"Hmm. This Mark fellow. Your step-dad, I take it."

"Yessir."

Christie shivered suddenly, as if a rabbit had walked over his grave. "You get in the car, boy. We got to go to town."

As they pulled out into the road, another car came barreling down the asphalt, twin points of light piercing the darkness. "Too fast for a road like this," Christie mumbled.

"It's Mark. I bet you it's Mark," Tam whispered.

Christie pulled out behind the other vehicle, heading the same way, much more slowly. Before they'd gone a mile, the car, now far ahead, braked, its taillights blooming scarlet, and whipped into a tight turn.

"Get down!" Christie said. He gripped the wheel so tightly his knuckles looked pale in the light from the dash. "He's checkin' us out."

The headlights went off, on again, off, as if signaling. Christie pulled to a halt beside the other car, while Tam crammed himself deep into the darkness beneath the dash. "You got problems?" Christie asked, his voice deep and untroubled.

"I'm looking for my son. The boy's run away, and his mother is just about out of her mind." Mark sounded convincing, even to Tam. "You see a kid about eleven come along the road some time around dusk?"

Christie rubbed his chin. "Seems as if I heard steps pass the house just before I sat down to supper. Didn't think much about it, though. Might have been him, I guess."

Tam could almost see Mark's face, the square chin, the chilly eyes, the ingratiating smile that had taken in smarter people than Mr. Christie. Mama, for instance.

But Christie said nothing more. Mark passed them, turned in the road, and headed toward town again.

"I guess we better take the turn up ahead and go to Lampkin," Christie said. "The sheriff's there, anyway. That bastard's goin' to have everybody in Stewartsville lookin' for you. We got to get that piece of cloth to somebody who'll look into this."

Tam scrootched out from his hiding place and sat again, staring at the craggy profile. "I thought you didn't like my family, Mr. Christie. Why're you helping me?"

"Your granddad wouldn't let me court Ruth," he said. "If he had've, I'd of been your daddy. Let's move, son. Anybody who's killed Ruthie has got to pay."

Tam heaved a long breath of relief. He kept a sharp eye on the road, wondering if Mark would turn back again, but they saw nothing before they took the Lampkin turn and set off on the twenty-mile drive to the county seat.

They were speeding along between ranks of tall trees, through the state forest, when Tam had a sudden thought. "Mr. Christie," he said, touching the old man's elbow. Mr. Christie, "I think you better stop and let me out. I think—I think he's probably turned again and is after us. And he's dangerous."

Christie didn't put on the brakes, but he let the car glide to a halt. "You go out the window so the dome light won't go on," he said. "I got the same feelin'...he's back there, coming hell bent for leather. You go hide, and I'll try to make it to Lampkin.

"Here, you take half that cloth and I'll take the other half, so's there's blood on both. That way, each of us'll have proof, if he gets one of us. We're just east of the historical marker. Don't you go gettin' lost, you hear?"

Then Tam was out of the window, standing beside the road. Christie looked at him, shrugged off his wool jacket, and shoved it out to him. "You need this more than I do. Now skedaddle."

Tam wrapped the warm jacket around him, finding that it came down almost to his ankles. He stumbled across the shoulder and into the bushes fringing the wood. The ground was damp, but he found a spot covered with pine needles, under a huge pine and walled in by a huckleberry thicket. He covered himself, head to heels, with the thick wool and closed his eyes.

Then he opened them again, thinking hard. If Mark caught up with Christie, he might ram the old car and take the evidence from the older man. Mark was strong. He could do it, if he wanted to. Somebody needed to stop him, to give Christie time to get to Lampkin and hand over the cloth to the sheriff.

There was nobody else. Just Tam. And it was his mother lying dead back there. Sighing, the boy crawled out of the thicket, leaving the betraying jacket behind, and headed for the highway. As he reached the shoulder, twin beams shot over the low hill and pinpointed him in their glare. Mark, almost certainly.

Tam clenched his fists in his pockets and drew a long breath. He had to stand here, his body hiding the marble historical marker. If that was somebody else, maybe they'd stop and help. If it was Mark—well, if this was what it took to avenge Mama, that was all right, too. He didn't stir as the car bulleted toward him, swerved to the shoulder, and crunched him against the deep-set marker, which screamed against the metal as if voicing Tam's own pain and terror.

Then it was all over, and he was rising above the tumble of broken marble and crumpled metal. A flicker of fire began to show its tongue beneath the hood, and the drifting boy could see the trapped man struggling to free himself. Then Tam laughed, though he had no voice.

The engine had rammed right back into Mark's lap. He was trapped there, and he would burn. There was no other car within sight, Tam saw as he rose higher and higher above the trees.

"Mama?" he thought into the cold emptiness of the sky. "Mama, I killed him for you."

There was no reply. It didn't matter; he had done what he wanted to do, and what happened now was not terribly important, whatever it might be that came after you died.

I have helped to butcher chickens, beef calves, armadillos, and pigs. For FOOD, badly needed food. I have no taste for killing animals for other reasons, particularly when one goes out into the woods to find critters that are defenseless. I've always wanted to arm the deer....

WHO STALKS THE STALKER?

Tod Lowe hitched his deer rifle under his elbow and slipped through the bushes, taking care not to make a lot of noise. The deer stand was dead ahead, he thought, beyond the big hickory. This year, for certain, he'd get his buck.

Last year—he grimaced as he worked his way through a tangle of brier vines—he'd shot four does and had had to leave them to rot in the woods. The law had become very strict about that, and none of the meat locker people would dress out a doe. Worse yet, they'd call the Game Warden on you, if you brought one in.

Something moved off to his left. He stopped in his tracks and listened. Deer, most likely. If he kept shooting them, he'd sooner or later get that buck. He'd bet Luther Jardin twenty dollars that he'd make it this year, and he intended to collect.

Another small sound came out of the huckleberry thicket, farther away this time, but still well within range. He snapped off a quick shot, and the heavy rifle boomed in his ears. There was a howl of pain, and a big dog shot away across a clearing, blood dripping from its shoulder, where the slug had creased it.

Damn! Just a dog. He'd had a bellyful of dogs, since old man Lynch, a couple of years back, sued him and won a potful of money because Tod killed one of his registered hounds. All right, the dog was on Lynch's property, confined by a mesh fence, but still, did that justify putting a damn animal above a man's right to hunt?

He moved forward again, more slowly. If he shot again, he'd scare away every deer in this area. No, he'd better take up his position on the stand and look down. Then he'd hit what he wanted, without frightening something he might want to kill.

The stand was a rude platform laid across three high branches of a hickory tree. Spikes had been driven into the thick trunk at wide intervals, making an awkward but effective ladder. Tod started up, his rifle slung over his shoulder.

He hated to work so hard—a man ought to be able to stand flat on the ground and shoot until he got his mark, but the fool Legislature had kept making game laws until it was plumb crazy. Looked as if they cared more for varmints than for taxpayers.

He hitched his butt onto the platform and set his feet on the branch that angled away just below it, his breath coming hard after the climb. He checked the load of his rifle, took off the safety, and laid the weapon across his knees.

The wood was a patchwork of brown and gold and gray-tan and purplish shadows below his perch. He could see a big rabbit mooching along, nibbling shoots of grass that had come up since the last rain. A covey of quail chittered in a patch of scrub, barely visible against the mottled leaves. He ought to bring his shotgun, next time, and take home some quail too. But now he waited, his gaze probing every shadow, every movement.

When the buck came into view, he could hardly believe it. This was a big one, old—he couldn't count the number of points, but the spread of antlers was impressive. He raised the rifle, took careful aim. From somewhere at a distance, there came a shot, and his own finger clamped down on the trigger.

Something powerful struck him out of the tree, sending him flailing and flopping into the scrub where the quail scattered in a thunder of wings. *What?* Tod wondered, in the brief moment before his life winked out.

* * * * * * *

Isaiah Lewis ejected the spent cartridge and set the safety. His 1903 Springfield might be old-fashioned and out-of-date, but it could still kill, just like it had done in a couple of World Wars.

He pocketed the retrieved cartridge casing without disturbing anything around him. He lived in the woods like an Indian, taking what he needed and no more, leaving things so unmarked that nobody looking for a trace of the one who killed that bastard over there would ever know he'd been here at all.

His feet were shod in moccasins that didn't leave sharp-edged marks in soft earth. They didn't even crumble the dead leaves underfoot as he backed easily out of his covert behind a dead snag and moved away, bending and twisting to miss the tangles of thicket and vine and young growth that crowded this cut-over forest.

Deer went this way. Men didn't, because they couldn't walk upright. He had learned through close observation that those who came here to hunt or to cut timber or just to amble through the trees didn't recognize any path that wasn't suited to humankind. So he had the freedom of the deer trails, which made an intricate network through this big tract, without fear that any hunter for man or animal would ever look closely at any path he chose.

More quickly than anyone unfamiliar with the old man's habits would have believed, he was far from the spot where he had killed the hunter. Now he moved surely over easy country, where scrub was shaded out by huge oaks, sweetgums, ashes, and hickories, with occasional pines lending thick carpets of straw to further conceal any track he might make.

The sun, even on a clear day, seldom could reach more than a few skinny fingers through the interlaced branches high above, and little vegetation interrupted the carpet of leaf-mold that cushioned his steps. When he returned to his home, he never took exactly the same route twice, understanding that even the softest footfalls could eventually create a trail that a skilled tracker might detect.

This time he dropped down beside the creek that ran, farther down, into the river that meandered through this wooded country. As he picked his way along the rabbit trails networking the bank, he thought about his victim. He had seen, last winter, the kill he had left to rot. Does all, and pregnant.

"The man might have had a family," he murmured, over the babble of a little waterfall. "He might have children."

The other Isaiah grunted. "If he wanted to be a good family man, why didn't he stay home and be one?" he asked himself. "Nobody made him come out here and bloody up the woods. Nobody made him waste all that meat. Damn idiot just felt big, with his high-powered gun and his expensive boots. Had to kill somethin', whatever it might be. I heard him shoot, and I heard a dog yelp. Careless. Careless. And that can get you killed."

He paused and grinned. He recalled, for the first time, the shot he had heard echoing his own. The bastard's finger was on the trigger—he must have pulled it when the slug hit him. The gun had discharged. He'd fallen from the tree. More than likely the sheriff would find this an accidental shooting. Lots of those happened during deer season.

* * * * * * *

When Lee Collins heard about Tod's death it hit him hard. They'd been boys together at Green Creek School, and though they hadn't been too close as men, they still shared a love of hunting. This was the week they'd planned to go together to Tod's special hunting spot, where he bragged about killing a buck every season, though often he didn't offer any proof of his claims.

At first, Lee thought he'd skip hunting this Saturday. But then he decided that old Tod wouldn't want that. What better proof of their long friendship could there be than going out and killing a buck in honor of his dead chum?

Sally had protested. "It isn't civilized! Here's poor Tod not cold in his grave, and you go out and shoot some little animal that never did you any harm. Why not go over and see Nellie, along with me? We can take her a casserole and one of my philodendron plants. After the funeral is when folks tend to forget about the bereaved."

Women! Casseroles and flowers were all they could come up with. Men, now, knew what other men valued, and he knew Tod would be with him in spirit while he waited to spot his prey. He had no idea what part of the river bottoms old Tod had claimed as his special place, but Lee had a spot of his own. Down near the post-oak glades was a little ridge from which you could see a long distance. Browsing deer showed up well, and there he intended to shoot his memorial to Tod.

* * * * * * *

Isaiah had been quartering his territory, looking for another invader. He suspected the sheriff must have taken the expected course, for nobody had searched the woods for any sign of another hunter, even. Discharged gun plus dead hunter equaled hunting accident. Case closed.

He grinned. Back in the days when he taught school, he'd learned to read people accurately. Young'uns were not that much different from men, just didn't have as much experience at hiding things. Once you knew what to look for, it was easy to spot it in adults as well.

No, he'd taught Sheriff Joe Higgins a ways back, and he'd scamped everything then too. Copied blurbs off book covers for reports, not to mention copying other things that Isaiah hadn't been able to nail him with. He'd let this go.

Sure as hell, the game wardens weren't going to be paying attention to what went on here along the river. Last fall they'd been shot up by a bunch of illegal net-setters, and they were sticking close to the lake and the national forest, trying to catch them again. With the drastic die-off of deer this year, it was up to Isaiah himself to keep those stupid, beer-guzzling bastards from town from killing the few animals left in the woods.

So he set off toward the ridge that overlooked the river, knowing it was a favorite spot for town-based hunters. You could see 'em up there, thinking they were hid in the skimpy growth of cut-over pines and post-oaks. They stuck up like the targets in a shooting gallery.

* * * * * * *

It had been a wet fall, and Lee's boots were clogged with mud before he reached his usual stand. He dropped to sit on a rock beneath a post-oak and used a stick to poke at the thick black mud on heels and soles. When he had lightened that load a bit, he climbed slowly and awkwardly up the ladder into the box-like deer stand he'd used for years.

It was still early, and fog draped itself over the low-lying country flanking the ridge. Ghostly shapes loomed out of the pearly mist, but he knew they were the tops of the huge pines and hardwoods growing along the river. It was too wet and too remote down here for the loggers to be able to work their big trucks in and out.

After a while the mist began to lift, and he saw a tawny shape, small and fleet, dash across from one patch of fog to another. There they were! He straightened his back, braced himself, and took aim, waiting for another to make the run.

He didn't hear the shot. Something hit him in the side and toppled him off the stand, and even as he fell he wondered how he'd managed to shoot himself. Then he knew. Somebody else had potted him, well and truly.

He could feel blood trickling from the corner of his mouth. Something in his chest whistled as he tried to breathe. Then he passed out, and he never came to again.

MYSTERY KILLER STALKS HUNTERS
AUTHORITIES ADMIT NO LEADS

From time to time Isaiah went to town and bought a newspaper. He put it off for a couple of days, just to be on the safe side, before looking into the results of his activities. Those headlines made him chuckle. He knew damn well there were no leads. There wasn't a woodsman worth the name in the sheriff's department. Hell, there wasn't a soul who could track King Kong through a mud puddle! And even if they'd hired somebody who could, there were no tracks, no traces left near the sites of the "accidents" or anyplace else.

Isaiah Lewis knew the woods. His grandparents had raised him there, and they were both part Cherokee, part Chickasaw. What they didn't know about the forest life wasn't worth knowing, and that blood tie had brought him back to the river bottom country, after he'd learned that teaching spoiled children of white men was a losing proposition.

As long as the white-eyes stayed where they belonged, he had no problem with them. His hut was hidden on a ridge and surrounded by swamp. Nobody who didn't understand the intricate maze of underwater foot-paths could get there without falling in and either drowning or getting snake-bit.

Armed with his newspaper and a couple of westerns off the rack, he turned back toward home. Let them stew. He'd get more of the nitwits before he was done. And nobody would ever know he was here at all.

Funny thing—most men don't believe it when you tell them never to harm a woman's children.

STALKING-WOMAN

She broke her first knife on the shell of the Turtle-Man she caught relieving himself behind a clump of huckleberry bushes. Squatting as he was, the blade should have slipped neatly between his shoulder blades and into his heart from behind...but the hard stuff that encased his torso snapped the flint, leaving her with a stub.

If the man had not been entangled with his own clothing, that would not have been enough. As it was, she made a rough job of his jugular before he could do anything about it. The knife, however, was lost. Only the fact that her victim carried one of bright metal, worth any number of hers, comforted her for its loss. She used the new weapon to sever one of the ears, which she strung on the thong she had brought for such a purpose.

The first of her son's killers now anchored the string of ears that she hoped to live to lay on the mound covering his burial place. There were now only five more to catch and to kill, in order to complete her tally of vengeance.

She did not remain in the thicket. The others would come to find their lost companion. She slipped backward through the brush, replacing every disturbed leaf or twig as she went. One of her own kind would be able to see where she had gone, but these blind newcomers would not, she felt certain.

Moving in a wide arc, she slid through the trees, down a shallow creek to pass the point nearest the campfire where the other Turtle-Men talked in their strange tongue, and around to a thick cluster of sumac on the side opposite that in which the body lay. Only one of these remaining men had taken part in the death of her son, and she waited only to get him apart from his fellows. Then she would leave these survivors to their own devices, and follow the group in which the other three traveled.

It was some time before one of the men called out for the other. *"Capitán! Capitán Escobedo! Cómo está usted?"*

The tallest of the armored figures stood, when there was no reply, and said something to his fellows. When he strode away through the bushes and disappeared behind the trees, Nahadichka flattened herself among the dead leaves and waited.

In just a moment, there came an exclamation, followed by a cry of *"¡Venga! ¡Venga! ¡El es muerto! ¡Aquí!"*

As the other three men rose to their feet, dropping the gear they had been mending while they rested, Nahadichka stared hard at the back of the one they called Ho-an. It had been he who caught her son as he played with the bright metal things he had found in the shelter of the white men. He had beaten the child, for Bear-boy had lived long enough to speak to his mother.

"The one whose hair burns, he caught me and beat me. And then the others came, and they beat me too. And why? I had not taken those things away. I only wanted to look at them." His dark eyes had been filled with astonishment, even as he died.

She had not been able to tell him. She only hoped, as she stalked those who had killed him, that they were as puzzled about the death that tracked after them as her son had been.

She furrowed her brow, staring, staring at the back of the man whose hair flamed in the firelight. As his companions crashed away toward the call for help, he turned, as if unwillingly, to gaze into the circle of brush about the small clearing.

"¡Juan! ¡Juan! ¡Aquí!" came the call again, and he shrugged and turned to go.

She was upon him before he knew what had happened. Her arm locked about his neck from behind, and that sharp steel knife that had belonged to his fellow parted the flesh of his neck smoothly, deliciously. He fell at her feet, and she stared down for an instant before leaning over to sever a circle of scalp, with its bright hair hanging long from it. That joined his ear on her string, once she regained the shelter of the forest that covered East Texas from the Big Water to the Flat Ground.

She did not wait to see what the three survivors might do. They were no concern of hers. That other group had been going west, and they now had two days on their road, while she had stalked this group. That much larger number of armored men would be harder to deal with, she was sure, and so she had made certain of this manageable one.

The deer-things that the Spaniards rode moved fast, and Nahadichka traveled most of the night, pausing only to chew some dried meat and to rest for a very short time. She ran through the trees, making shortcuts when the ancient trail followed by her prey made one of its curves to avoid difficult ground or deep streams. One afoot could go where those awkward beasts could not.

She felt that those ahead of her could not know that they were pursued. She had seen how they regarded her people, and the women they had scorned as of no account, much to the amusement of the entire tribe. Her people knew all too well that without the work of the women life would have been almost impossible. Men liked to hunt and to fish and to battle among themselves, but they were not at all dependable when it came to farming and preparing hides and making the stores of food that kept the People alive in winter.

So the Turtle-Men would not expect to be stalked by the mother of the child they had beaten to death. That thought helped her to keep her wearying feet moving at top speed. It woke her from her brief bouts of exhausted sleep, and it bore her up as she crossed the rivers, in which alligators sometimes lay sluggishly, watching as she swam or waded or walked over fallen trees.

Her people had traveled all the forest country for countless generations. Their trails were many, though that oldest of roads that the Spaniards used was the best marked and easiest. Nahadichka knew others, however, that criss-crossed the forests, linking up bits of other tracks, sometimes faster to travel than that easier road. She used them, making a wide angle southwestward that brought her out of the woodlands in less than two more days.

When she examined the trail of the Old Ones, there were no tracks of the hooves of the beasts, no droppings in neat piles. She had beaten her prey to this point, and she knew they were still in the forest country. Something inside her relaxed, as she found a spot from which she could see the track without being seen and slept, her ear flat to the ground, for a long while.

There was no vibration of hoof on earth to wake her, and when she rose it was with her strength renewed. She took up an easy trot, again along a minor set of trails, that sent her again into the forests. She watched the crows, the circling hawks, as she ran, and at last, before the sun was overhead, she heard a raucous chorus of caws from the direction of the road.

It wasn't difficult to keep her prey in sight without being seen. Those Turtle-Men were as blind as new puppies. She kept pace with the group, staying well downwind of them. She could track them by the stink of their rank bodies, as well as the strong scent of the beasts they rode.

She felt sure they would camp before darkness fell, for a convenient stream offered a comfortable site. They were a people who liked their ease, as her People had learned by watching them. She scurried ahead and found herself a spot in which to rest and wait, with the stream and the clearing edging it within easy distance.

They were noisy and careless. Their beasts made their whinnying noises as they neared the water, and the men shouted in their coarse voices as they made their camp. She felt nothing but contempt for them. Children were valuable, and these creatures thought nothing of killing one, simply because he was curious. The thought made her dry eyes burn with rage, as she slid through the tangle of brush along the edge of the water and found a spot from which to watch them.

There was no moon that night, which was helpful. Their watchfire flared red against the darkness, and the four sentries thumped about the perimeter of the camp, as easy to hear as the crackle of the flames. She had marked, while they cooked and ate and sat about the fire, the three she wanted. One had gone into the shelter they set up at the farther edge of the clearing. Two were together in one nearer the fire. The four shelters held three hands of men, though they took turns watching through the night.

Nahadichka crept easily around the circle, avoiding the sentries without effort. Their heavy feet, their audible breathing, and their occasional comments as they met and passed made them irrelevant. She reached the dark tangle of grapevine and sweetgum and oak and hickory for which she had aimed herself, and then she lay waiting for a chance to slip across the narrow span of grass to the shelter.

The fire burned down, and the shadows grew darker. She found her chance and reached the side of the shelter without trouble. Her keen blade made a long slit, soundlessly, in the stuff, allowing her to peer through.

Three men lay cramped together in the narrow space. The flap was thrown back, and by the flicker of the coals outside, she could see them. The long one—that was the one she wanted! The others she would leave as they were, for they would fear greatly, and that was worse than death.

The knife moved, slick and silent, and the long legs flexed, straightened, twitched. She took the ear and slipped backward again, into the concealing forest. There was another camping spot, a day's travel westward. She would be waiting there.

* * * * * * *

The next camp the group made was much more secure than the first. She watched them from a clump of brush as they cut away encroaching growth that might conceal an enemy. The horses were hobbled, and six sentries patrolled the perimeter, instead of three. The men kept their metal shells on their backs, instead of setting them aside for comfort, and a few even kept their heads covered with the high metal pots they wore.

She found herself able to laugh quietly at the obvious nervousness of the group. When an owl mourned shrilly downstream, they all jerked and turned to stare. She found that very gratifying. She was making them suffer.

There was no way to reach either of the others as she had done their fellow, and so she did not wait for full darkness. Again, a man went behind a clump of brush to relieve himself. He was not one she wanted, so she waited patiently until he was done. After a time another came, his sword in his hand, his gaze flicking from right to left, before and behind him. She lay curled around her bush, secure in the knowledge that he was as blind as his fellows.

When he had his clothing all undone and disarranged, she uncurled silently, slithered over the ground as quietly as a rattlesnake, and took him from behind. Having learned with her first attempt, she went for the throat, always, knowing that the armor would foil a stab at the back. He died as easily as the others had done, and she dropped him into his own mess and retired downstream, crossed the water, and sped southward and westward, paralleling the old road.

Only one of the killers was left alive. She told herself that she should be satisfied, should return through the forest to her own Caddoan people while yet she could. Her stealth and cunning had been great, but she knew that fortune had favored her as well. You could not depend upon that to continue.

Yet every time she thought to turn back, her son's bewildered eyes stared at her from the leafy crowns of the trees or the muddy purls of the river water. No, she must go on to complete the task she had taken upon herself. She did not wait for the Spaniards to camp, this last time. She knew they would be so cautious that there would be little chance for success. She must attack from some hidden place, at a time when they least expected it. That meant that she could not use a stream or a river as her hiding place. They would now expect that.

She must rise from the earth itself, ready to kill that last slayer, whatever happened to her. Nahadichka was a woman of the forest now, but she had been born in the plains of a warrior people. She knew how to mislead an enemy into thinking himself safe, and she set about doing that.

The forest had been damp, for there had been rain in the east. But the flatlands were much dryer, and the grass, the soil, and the bushes and scrub oaks were dusty. She became a heap of dusty weeds beside the faint track that generations of travelers had worn into the prairie.

The sun burned up the east, traveled overhead slowly, and at last she heard the thud of hooves through the earth against which she lay. The group came closer, and she opened her eyes to stare through the mesh of grass she had arranged so as to hide her face. First came the heavy man who led the Turtle-Men. Then the one in black robes who raised his hands so often.

Behind came the others, riding in pairs, their hands on their weapons and their eyes busy studying the terrain about them. They were not fools, those Spaniards.

The last of the killers rode on the side nearest her. Fortune still was kind. Two pairs rode before him and three behind. There would be time. As he drew nearer, she gathered herself into a tense knot of muscle and resolve. The horse stepped steadily forward, and she sprang upright almost beneath its hooves. The knife flew unerringly from her hand and buried itself to the hilt in the eye socket of her victim.

There was a circle of riders about her, weapons in hand, their eyes burning with anger. Anger and astonishment. *"¿Una mujer? ¡No lo creo! ¿Donde están los hombres?"* Their words meant nothing to her.

She stood proudly, waiting, as several of the riders pulled away and circled, wider and wider, searching, she suspected, for a band of warriors that had harried them across the countryside. She smiled as the blade swung, holding her neck still for its impact.

Her son was avenged, and she had no other child. Her man had two wives to comfort him. It was time to die.

She felt the impact of the blade—and then the darkness descended, and she was freed of effort. The string of ears would not go onto her son's mound, but perhaps she would find Bear-boy there in the Other Place, where the deer were fat, and the fruit was sweet and plentiful.

That would be enough.

Rednecks sometimes still have erroneous ideas about the vulnerability of females they meet...BIG MISTAKE!

A MOST GENTEEL PURSUIT

I never thought I could be talked into an extended leave of absence, not even after being beaten into hamburger by a bunch of street kids with bicycle chains. My work is what I am, and when I'm off, it leaves me restless and adrift. Once I got out of the hospital, I meant to go right back onto the streets, but two big obstacles stood in my way.

My grandmother was the bigger of the pair. She didn't like it when I was accepted into police training. She didn't dislike police, but she thought that was no job for her granddaughter. She was terrified every time I left the house, and prayed hard while I was away at work. After the beating, she showed signs of going into cardiac arrest when I mentioned going back on duty.

The other obstacle was my doctor, who shook his head and looked grim every time I mentioned going back to work. "You don't think so now, but this has been a strain on you. It will take a while to build your strength again. You lost a lot of blood, almost as much tissue, and your body has to rebuild itself. You need to sit back and eat your grandmother's cooking for a while. Those scars need to heal."

Between them, they got me to agree to some time off. I almost went crazy sitting at the window, watching cars pass on the freeway and wishing I was out there to pull them over for speeding. Gramma realized, after a while, that I couldn't bear being lazy.

"Let's go up to the old place on the river," she said at last. "I'll call Cousin Cindy to get somebody to clean up the house and get the utilities connected. You always liked the farm and the woods and the river, and that'll give you something to do. Maybe you might take your paints—you used to be really good with watercolors. I wish...," but she didn't finish.

She was right, I had been good. Maybe I'd pick up the habit while I was off-duty. It was a relaxing pastime, if nothing else.

I went shopping for supplies. A pocket watercolor kit, a pad of 130-pound watercolor paper, a folding stool, and I was ready for business. I still had my brushes, carefully cleaned and put away. By the time we were on our way, I was really getting excited about painting. I like doing birds and landscapes and tumble-down houses. God knows, there are enough of all those in East Texas to keep me busy for years.

I realized, as it began to melt away with the miles, that I'd been pushing a dull weight of anger deeper and deeper inside me since the attack. It had lessened, but I knew it was still there. The police psychologist told me it would stay with me for a long time. Maybe forever. I knew all about that: after my divorce I'd been furious for five years, and even now it didn't do to think about it often.

Gramma and I moved back into her old home as if we'd never been gone. She and Gramps raised me, my sister, and my brother there after our parents were killed, and they did a bang-up job. We had what we needed, including lots of love and the kind of discipline you don't find much any more, firm but fair.

As usual, Gramma had known just what I needed. She'd told me, years before, that if I didn't divorce Reed I'd end up killing him (or he'd kill me). She was right.

After Gramps died, she came to Houston, though she hated the city, and kept house for me. Now that she'd put me back in the woods, I knew I'd been missing that for years.

I dived into the thick stands of forest like a fox and renewed my acquaintance with favorite places and familiar creatures. I began taking my painting stuff with me, for it all folded and packed into a neat shape to be carried on my shoulders. I started with quick sketches of birds. That wasn't enough, and soon I was considering landscapes.

There was a wide eddy where the river curved to the east. The woods came down to the banks on one side, amid cattails, waterweed, and button willows. The larger species of willows bent over the water, their reflected shapes warped by the ripples.

I wanted to paint it in watercolor, using that as a sketch from which to do a big oil later, when I was at home again. I'd take part of the home country back to Houston with me to cover my living room wall.

I did the preliminary sketches, got the composition just right, and started on my real work. Coming in after a shift on the streets, I could gaze into that picture and let all the hostility drain out of me.

For three days I sat on my stool on the sandy point above the eddy, getting every detail right before touching brush to water.

On the fourth day it rained. I sat at the window, impatient for it to clear. When it did I was back there on my stool, as soon as the light reached the angle I wanted. I washed in the values of forest and water and felt the old power run through my fingers into the brush.

A motor muttered around the bend, and a boat came into sight, wrinkling the water. It sputtered to a stop and a voice yelled, "Whatcha doin'?"

The biggest of the four men, the one who yelled, was a red-faced jerk who wouldn't have understood if I told him. I held my temper, however.

"I am painting the river. In watercolor." My tone was sharp, but it was the best I could do.

The three younger men looked blank, but the questioner seemed to think I was making fun of him. "I asked you a civil question," he bellowed.

"I gave you an accurate answer," I said. "I want a picture of that bend to hang on my wall. To get it, I have to paint it. Simple, even for you, I'd think." It wasn't particularly diplomatic, but I was on my grandmother's land, in a place that had never seemed dangerous in all my thirty years.

I dipped my brush into the paint and laid in a ragged line to create the shadow beneath the farther bank. When I looked up, the four had come ashore and were moving toward me, lined up between me and the water.

"What in the world do you want?" I asked the red-faced man.

"Just a little roll in the hay," he said, showing big buck teeth. "This time it'll be mud, but you can't have everything. It's a waste, letting a pretty woman set out in the woods with nothin' better to do than smear paint around. We'll show you a real good time...." I didn't wait for the rest. I rose off the stool and got ready. They looked surprised, but they kept moving toward me, almost within reach.

"Now don't get feisty, honey. There's nothin' you kin do—nobody's closer than about five miles downriver. We won't hurt you, just have a good time, all together." The idiot really believed that. I could see it in his mud-colored eyes and the smirk on his face.

He lunged toward me and caught my shirt, tearing it off with one tug. Then he saw my scars.

While the bicycle chains had missed my face, they'd made a real job on my torso. Like I said, I looked like hamburger when my fellow officers found me.

"My lord!" said Red-Face. "What happened to you?"

The fury that had been buried was boiling to the surface. These four rednecks thought the finest thing a woman could hope for was to be gang-raped in the woods, and that assumption had triggered something deep inside me. I had thought I could control it, but I found I couldn't.

I'd been taught hand-to-hand combat by the best. Two of the men went flying into the river under my first attack, without ever knowing what hit them. The other youngster took one look at me and dived in without help. But Red-Face was one of the old school who thought a woman couldn't possibly handle him. He got redder than ever and opened his beefy arms to get me in a bear-hug.

I went for his eyes with my right hand, while I tangled my left leg with his right and pushed him down into the mud. He gave a yell and put his hands over his fingernail-stabbed eyeballs. Tears leaked through his fingers, mixed with a bit of blood.

I rolled to my feet and caught him by the collar. Dragging him along the bank, aided by the slick mud, I dumped him into the boat, where his soaked companions were already waiting, very quietly. They pulled him in and looked up at me with fear in their eyes.

With one foot, I shoved the boat free of the bank. I grabbed up my torn shirt and tied it around me, while they drifted out into the river. The anger was subsiding now, leaving a feeling of peace behind it.

I called after them, "You boys better get used to the idea that you can't just take what you want. It's not safe, with men or women, any more. Don't come to Houston, by the way." They were far enough now so I yelled, "Down there, I'm a cop!"

Three heads turned to look back. The fourth raised itself from the bottom of the boat and looked too. His eyes were already clearing. Then somebody pulled the starter cord, and the motor sputtered, caught, and revved ruinously. They rocketed out of sight.

I put my painting gear back into order and sat down whistling. The world was brighter than it had seemed in quite a while. That undercurrent of anger was no longer simmering inside me. I had needed a good, fair fight, not the ambush those street kids had set up.

Now I'd had it, and it felt great. Nobody had lasting damage, except to macho egos, though for a minute I'd had the impulse to blind that redneck, though I'd pulled my punch.

I painted until the light failed. Then I went whistling home through the woods. Gramma met me with food ready on the table. "You look so well, dear. But how did you tear your shirt?" she asked. Without waiting for a reply, she went on, "I'm so glad you went back to painting. It's such a genteel pursuit."

I didn't quite laugh aloud, though I chuckled internally most of the evening. Then I slept like a baby, while the whippoorwills and the hoot owls and the crickets filled the night with music.

Wild hogs range the East Texas woods, and more than one who has run afoul of them has never lived to tell of it....

THIS LITTLE PIGGY...

The wood was ripe with autumn, the sugary scent of fallen leaves mingling with the tang of pine that had felt the first nip of frost. Beneath his feet, Rob felt the satisfactory scrunch of golden hickory leaves that ruffled about his ankles as he waded through them.

Occasionally he stooped to pick up a nut, still clasped tightly in its green-brown husk. Merrily made hickory-nut cakes for Christmas, though it was a royal pain to shell the suckers. He and the kids mashed fingers and pricked themselves with nut-picks, but it was all a part of the Christmas magic his wife managed to make it from what they could forage for themselves. Soon it would be time to bring the whole family, baskets in hand, to the hickory wood and gather their winter store.

There was a scuffled trail through the yellow-brown layer of leaves. He stooped to examine the tracks, noting the marks of many cleft hooves. Wild pigs were already at the mast, and if his family was to get its share they'd better hurry.

A bellow in the distance brought him upright again, and he swung his polished stick as he strode off through the thick woods toward the sound. Old Hassie was having her calf, and as usual she had hidden herself well and truly and then had trouble delivering it. You'd think she'd catch on, sooner or later. But then, a cow's mind worked different from a man's, and that was a fact.

The morning was brilliant with sun blazing in a polished cobalt sky. The treetops leaned above him, rustling in the light breeze that held the coolness of East Texas fall weather, and the path stretched ahead like the Yellow-Brick Road. Rob began to whistle. On such a day it was a joy just being alive.

This was a very old part of the wood, where the woodcutters of his father's youth had never gone. His grandfather particularly loved the towering hickories and gums and oaks and ashes that formed it. He had visited here every spring, bringing whatever grandchild he could round up to smile gently at the jacks-in-the-pulpit that grew in the damp spot where the creek bank was low. Those were good memories, and Rob was glad that this forty-acre patch of the farm had escaped the ravages that messed up the woods all over the rest of the county.

There were deer in the thickets around him, though he never saw them, just their tracks that overlapped his when he returned the way he came. There were coyotes that ranged down the creek, and from time to time a cougar-track marked the mud in the flat or obliterated a cowpat in a pasture. Rob liked to think of those creatures still surviving because of his uncut land and his hard line with hunters.

Then there were the piney-woods rooters, the wild pigs that were natural to this area. They were bigger than they used to be, because of domestic hogs that escaped and went free with their wild kindred. There were numbers of them in the cutover woods of neighboring farms and more along the river where old forest still remained.

It looked as if he was getting his share too, for the sharp tracks had chewed up the cow trail he was following. If they started getting into Merrily's garden, he'd have to do something, though he hated to shoot anything since Vietnam.

Another bellow hurried him again, and in ten minutes he had located the thicket in which Hassie stood, head down, sides straining, eyes staring at him reproachfully. Sighing, Rob patted her and scratched behind her horns. Then he went behind and saw the problem. One leg of the calf had bent at an awkward angle, preventing the body from emerging. He put on his rubber gloves, reached in and corrected the position, and the little heifer almost shot out into his arms, propelled by her mother's muscles.

Once relieved of her problem, Hassie turned and ate the afterbirth with absent-minded thoroughness, and began licking the calf from head to tail. That was that, thought Rob, picking up his stick and turning back into the wood.

As he had expected, deer tracks were pricked into the yellowish dust on top of his sneaker tracks. The little devils were curious as cats, but they were too shy to let you know they were there.

A bit farther along he noted that more pig tracks were there as well. And then he heard them, the muffled grunts, the patter of hooves, the crushing sound of many animals moving through drifts of leaves. They were heading his way, and since 'Nam, he couldn't run worth a damn.

Rob never carried a gun, for he didn't like shooting things. Even a snake, he often said, would leave you be if you stood still and gave him the chance. Oh, a water moccasin would sometimes be really nasty, but they were pretty slow and it wasn't that hard to get out of their way. Pigs were something else. He had a cousin who had lost two toes on her left foot to his grandfather's big sow after the visiting children climbed onto the hog-pen, bare feet thrust into cracks between the logs forming its fence. He could still hear Lily's incredulous shriek and see the sow chomping down on little-girl toes. That had made him extremely cautious in his dealings with porkers of all kinds.

Wild hogs made domesticated ones look like pussycats. Meeting a bunch of them in the woods with no weapon but a stick was not a good thing to do. If they were hungry, they'd eat a man or a dog or a calf as a mid-morning snack. He wished suddenly that he'd let Snap come with him. The big redbone hound had yowled pitifully when he left him tied, but when all was said and done, a cow with a new calf had nothing but suspicion for any dog, and Snap would have made his work harder.

Hogs were wary of dogs, however, and the hound could probably have gone baying up the path and scared this bunch into the next county. As it was, Rob knew it was best not to contest the way with them. Even the piglets could bite a plug out of a leg or a foot protected by nothing stronger than a sneaker, and a big boar could rip you, thigh to belly-button, with one swipe of his tusks.

He moved aside into a huckleberry thicket and looked about. This was no place to be trapped. He needed a tree to climb, for the trampling was getting very close, now, and the gruff comments between members of the troop sounded as if they were right at his elbow.

The crooked oak off to his left would be just right, though it was set a bit apart from the clump of ash and elm around it. There was a good spot to set his toe, and once up to the first branch he was in good shape. The leg that he'd had all but shot away in 'Nam wasn't any good for shinning up a tree trunk anymore.

He moved quickly through the bushes and into the space around the oak. Its top was still green, for live oaks lost their leaves only when new spring ones pushed them off the twigs.

He hugged the fat trunk, got his good toe into a notch, and sprang upward, grabbing a branch and swinging into the first crotch. There was a lot of room in the treetop, with many limbs conveniently spaced. He went as far up as was comfortable and then sat on a flat branch, hugging the trunk and watching the woods below his perch.

Fifteen wild pigs marched down the path, the boar at the head of the group, followed by three sows and eleven youngsters of various ages from yearlings to last summer's litter. That bunch could crunch up everything including his bones, leaving nothing to show he'd been here but his polished hickory stick.

He sat so quietly that a jaybird lit on the twig above his head and began preening. But a crow, passing overhead, saw the intruder in the tree and began yelling at the top of his voice, the warning sounding to every corner of the forest.

The boar down on the path paused, letting the rest of the family clump about him. The tusked head went up as the animal sniffed the air, peering short-sightedly about. Then the crow called again, and the boar turned off the track and came snuffling through the thicket to halt at the foot of the oak.

He looked up, and Rob, looking down, saw complete confidence in the hog's bearing. Nothing had ever escaped this beast's appetite, he realized with a sudden chill down the middles of his bones.

The younger pigs rooted about the oak, finding old acorns or grubs or rootlets. The sows flopped in the shade, grunting contentedly at this unexpected rest. The boar sat back on his haunches, his upper body propped up on his forelegs, and surveyed his prey with all the coolness of a hunter planning how to approach a covey of quail. It looked as if the family had settled in for as long as it took to do the job.

Why had he chosen a tree so far from the others? With that monster at his heels, Rob knew he could have gone up a straight wall, bad leg or no bad leg. He might have been able to follow a big branch to the next tree, and the one after that. As it was, he was stuck up here with no place to go but straight up. And nobody would know that something was wrong until milking time, when he didn't return from hunting Hassie.

In the fall, he was free once he'd put out the morning hay for the dairy cows. Merrily and he had an agreement—either could take some time off to ramble through the woods, if it didn't cause them to neglect anything important. She wouldn't think anything if he took all day, which it began to seem that he might.

The limb on which he sat got harder and harder, and he shifted along to put up his feet. His butt was numb, his skin scrubbed by the rough bark, and the sun was slowly moving down the west when

Rob began to think the animals below might well win this game.

They were comfortably on solid ground, with water close enough so they could visit the creek in shifts. They certainly showed no sign of giving up the siege and going wherever they had been headed when that damn crow warned them he was hiding in the oak.

On the other hand, his leg was giving him Billy Heck, and his bottom was all but destroyed by sitting on the rough rounds of branches. His neck was sunburned under the back of his cap, and he felt as if every bug in East Texas had taken up residence in his clothes.

This was not a fun day in the woods!

Shadows stretched long across the small clearing around the base of the oak. The sun moved down behind the line of trees that marked the distant course of the bigger stream into which his creek ran, and the sky to the east began to darken. Milking time, and he wasn't there.

Merrily would have things ready, the kids would be rounding up the milk cows, and they would all know that something had gone wrong, but they couldn't do a thing about it until they were through with the job at hand. The cows came first, no matter what.

He groaned and leaned his head against the trunk of the oak, hearing the chatter of breeze through the narrow leaves. He was getting cold. The wind was rising, bringing with it a brisk chill. He shivered, feeling the old wound in his leg twinge deeply. If he lived through the night, he'd be fit for the nursing home by morning, he thought.

Merrily had forty acres to search, and doing it at night would be a long job, unless he heard her coming and yelled, which it was beginning to be doubtful that he could do. He was falling asleep even as he thought about it. If he did that, he fell out of the tree, and that meant the immediate end of everything.

He could hear, almost subliminally, the distant throb of the compressor that powered the milking machine. The cows would be strolling up the chute into the barn, taking their places in the stalls, there in the warmth and light. The family could milk blindfolded, even Karen, his youngest, whose job was keeping the feed bins filled and the udders washed.

They'd survive, if he wound up being eaten by wild hogs. But he'd really have liked to see his three grow up, to be a grandparent with Merrily, to grow old on this piece of ground that his family had been granted back in the Spanish days. There came an irritable sound below, but now it was too dark to see anything but shadows where the hogs still waited for him to fall into their jaws. He wrapped both arms about the tree, closed his eyes, and tried to doze without relaxing too much. From time to time he woke with a jerk and listened.

Then there came a deep bark. Snap, back on the top of the hill west of the barn. Rob pursed his lips and tried to whistle, but his mouth was too dry. No sound came out but a feeble puff.

"Snap!" he tried to yell, but his throat was raw to cracking, and his effort was pretty pitiful.

Infuriated and now wide awake, he reached up and broke off a hand of twigs that had been tickling him all day. He flung it down among the black shadows, and a flurry of grunts rose to his ears.

"Snap!"

After a while there came a rush of paws through fallen leaves, the baying of a hound on the scent. Another shadowy shape dashed into the clearing. "Watch it, boy!" he called, this time making a bit more noise.

They'd eat his dog, if he didn't watch out. He reached for another leafy branch and twisted it off, to drop among those below. That distracted the swine a bit, but he couldn't tell what was happening. There was breathy growling and grunting and snuffling and a lot of unidentifiable sounds that only made Rob uneasy.

Then he saw a pair of lights moving beyond the trees. They bounced as the tractor crossed tree roots and holes, but they came on steadily, and now he could hear a voice.

"Rob! Ro-ob!" Merrily was coming.

Snap broke off his engagement with the boar and went yelling through the bushes. Rob saw him dash into the tractor lights, run in three circles, and head back for the clearing. After a brief pause, the tractor turned and followed, crushing thickets under its heavy, water-filled tires.

Then the scene below was brilliantly illuminated in the twin beams from the tractor. The boar stood, neck bristled, tusks gleaming, eyes sparking red in the glow. The young pigs scuttered into the undergrowth and disappeared; the sows, after surveying the situation, followed them.

The boar was the dangerous one, certain to kill calves or even children, given the chance. As badly as he hated to say it, Rob called down over the roar of the engine, "Shoot him, Hon! He's a bad one."

The 30.06 spoke, the shot echoing through the trees and away into the distance. The boar sank back onto his haunches; then he keeled over slowly and lay flat on his side, blood drooling into the dust of the rooted-up area. The rapid patter of retreating hooves marked the flight of his family into the forest.

Rob flexed his legs, finding that the bad left one still moved, though with considerable difficulty. Now a hand-light shone upward, lighting his way as he stepped down from branch to branch, holding for dear life in case the leg gave way entirely.

The tractor pulled up close to the tree, so he could step directly down onto a wheel. He fell into Merrily's arms, and she helped him settle into the hard seat, where he put his arms on the steering wheel and laid his head on them, dizzy with relief, hunger, and thirst.

"You okay?" she asked.

"Okay. But that's too much meat to let lie there for the coyotes. We can grind him up into sausage for the winter, if we can get him home. You think?"

The backwash of light made her pale face glow, and her smile was full of relief. "I shot him. I can load him on the trailer. It's back there in the trail, where I dumped it before taking off after Snap. Hold on here. Can you drive?"

"No." He was shaking now, with chill as much as exhaustion. "I think I'd better get down. With him."

It took a bit of doing but soon he sat in the dust beside the boar, holding the hand light to guide Merrily back with the trailer. He turned the beam onto the animal beside him, seeing the dark blood in the dust, the glazed eyes, the stark curves of the steely tusks. This animal had actually intended to eat him, and probably would have if Snap hadn't followed his trail.

Instead, he would feed Rob's family with pork sausage for much of the winter. Life was funny, whether you were a hog or a man. He wondered if others as dangerous as this one would come into his woods. The word was that wild pigs were growing in numbers from year to year.

Merrily had left the rifle beside him, and he took it into his lap. One thing was for certain: he'd never go into the woods again without protection. Principles were one thing; survival was another.

The tractor heaved into the clearing and Merrily backed the trailer almost to Rob's feet. Grabbing the iron brace that held the backboard, he hauled himself upright and laid the rifle carefully on the worn boards.

"Here piggee, piggee, piggee!" he whispered, as the two of them struggled to heave four hundred pounds of dead boar into their trailer. It wasn't easy, but it got done at last, and as they jounced away through the trees Rob looked back once at the dark space between the trees.

He'd entered it one sort of man. He was leaving it another.

Some of the innocence he thought he'd rediscovered after 'Nam had turned out to be foolish, and he gladly left it behind as they moved through the night toward their home. Behind them there came the long wail of a coyote, smelling blood, smelling death, coming to see if there was anything left for him, as their dangerous human presence moved away into the darkness.

The big woods are full of strange old ladies with odd habits. Revenge being a fine old backwoods tradition, this one made a hobby of it.

OLD WOMAN

It was hot. Evening was creeping through the river-bottom country, and tree-shadow filled the clearing around her house, but the steamy heat hadn't lifted a bit. Old Woman sat in the swing beneath her chinaberry tree, fanning vigorously with the cardboard fan that the Levi Garrett Snuff salesman had given her forty years before. Every time it went limp, over the long years, she stiffened it with starch and a hot iron, but it had been decades since she had seen the picture that decorated it.

A moth was dipping into the four o'clocks, unfurling his long proboscis to reach into the deep blossoms. A crow was punctuating the breathless quiet, when, out of no place, there came a hint of a cool breeze. The mockingbird in the elm struck up his evening song.

Old Woman sighed with satisfaction. She hadn't felt like exerting herself in the heat of the day, but now she did. And this was, she felt in her bones, THE NIGHT.

Old Rupe, lying among the four o'clocks, raised his hind leg and thoughtfully scratched at a flea. Then he turned his nose toward the lane leading into the forest and perked up one ear. She understood him as clearly as if he had spoken.

"Somebody coming along the path, eh?" she asked. "Good. Maybe it's the one I want to see, you think?"

The dog turned his faded brown eyes toward her and sighed as he laid his furry chin on his front paws. Not this time, his entire attitude told her.

"Oh, shoot!" she grunted. "Another of those giggly kids, I guess, wanting a fortune told. Dammit. I wonder why I ever started that foolishness. Such a bother, and on a hot evening too."

She rocked herself back and forth in the swing by the pressure of one toe against the ground. The breeze was now cool enough for comfort, and she put the fan carefully into her antique reticule, which lay beside her on the weathered wooden seat. From its depths, she took a bundle of crochet thread and a needle and began hooking rapidly into and out of the linen strand. A spidery doily, incongruously dainty, grew between her arthritic fingers.

Rupe, eyes closed, monitored the approach of the visitor by minute twitches of his ears. She knew to the minute when to put away her work and look up to greet the newcomer.

There were two of them, this time, both young girls, obviously sisters. The sound of giggling reached the swing before they came into view around the sharp bend in the lane. When they saw Old Woman waiting for them, they hushed instantly, their gray eyes going wide, their tow-heads cocking alertly.

"You'd run away again, if you dared," Old Woman said with satisfaction. "But you don't dare, so come into my yard and sit on the bench. What brings you out here into the woods, so late in the evening? As if I didn't know!"

The taller girl, perched nervously on the bench, glanced at the short lively one. "You tell her, Charlotte!"

The baby face scrunched up with concentration, as she cleared her throat. "At school, they told us you can see the future. Can you?" The question sounded more blunt than she had evidently intended. She looked a bit frightened.

Old Woman sighed. "Oh, I can, for what it's worth. Best thing God ever did for our kind was to leave us in ignorance, though. You sure and certain you want to go digging into things better left to time?"

Charlotte giggled automatically. "We do. Oh, yes, we surely do. Which of us will marry Jim Hollander? Just tell us that, and we won't ever have to fight about it again!"

Old Woman sighed. How many such sap-brained questions had been asked of her over the years? How many irrelevant visions had she conjured up to answer them? If her long-term purpose hadn't held her to her course, she would have given up this nonsense long ago.

"I don't do this for free, you know," she said.

"What do you charge?" asked the older girl, taking a coin purse from the pocket of her tight jeans. "We brought some money."

"I don't charge money," said Old Woman. "I live so far away, all alone, and I never get to town. Never see much of anybody. I ask people to run errands for me—nothing much at all. Just little things like giving messages to people."

The girl put the purse into her pocket. "Sure. Glad to. Just tell us what you want, and we'll do it."

Old Woman wondered if this wasn't a waste of time. Her instinct told her that he would come tonight, but she might as well be hanged for a goat as a sheep, she thought. "Tell Amos Harrington that I'm thinking about him," she said. "Tell him I haven't forgot, forty years or not, and that I have something for him, if he'll come down here to see me."

The sisters exchanged knowing glances. They knew all about love affairs, old and young, new and ancient. So the old lady had a lover forty years ago, Old Woman could see them thinking.

She smiled internally and said, "Come into the house. I need to stretch out, when I Vision myself. Even for a simple thing like this.... I'm not young anymore." She sighed, rose, and led the way into her pine-log cabin that hunkered like a sleeping animal at the back of the clearing. It was already dark inside. She lit a kerosene lamp and showed the sisters where to sit while she conjured up the Vision.

When she sat up again, she was chuckling silently, though she managed to sober her face before confronting the girls. "I hate to tell you this, young ladies, but neither of you will marry Jim. He's already got Lennie Miller in the family way, and her Daddy will make him marry her before the year's out. So there's no need for you to fuss any more about him—he's got a date with a shotgun by the end of October."

Charlotte jumped to her feet. "That two-timing...Helen, we've been wasting our time fussing and scratching and clawing, all for nothing!" She didn't look directly at Old Woman.

Helen, too, was on her feet. "Better to know now than to waste any more time." She turned to Old Woman. "We'll take your message. Maybe you'll be luckier than we were."

Old Woman returned to the yard and sat in the swing. The new moon was just above the trees, riding the tender turquoise of the evening sky as the last strands of color died from the west. A whip-poor-will was fluttering his plaintive cry from the hickory, and bull-frogs, crickets, and katydids were ratcheting and creaking high and low, in every tone from soprano to bass.

Rupe, a black shadow among the four o'clocks, raised his head, but only the rustle of the plants told her he had moved. She sat still, hidden by the chinaberry even from the pale light of the moon. To her right was the cover of the dry well, where a tumble of honey-suckle released its scent into the night air. A screech owl's cry trembled through the wood as footsteps padded in the powdery dust of the path and Rupe growled low in his throat.

She had left the lamp burning in the front room of the cabin, and its light made a ruddy track on the flagged path to the porch. The man passed her, silent in the swing, without knowing she was there. Even after forty years, she knew his step, and something inside her surged, hot and fierce, before it subsided into cold waiting.

She rose, still silently, and followed as he mounted the porch and tapped on the sagging screen door. "Old Woman! Old Woman! Why do you keep sending word for me to come? Now I have, and you can quit pestering me for something that was done with forty years ago. Something nobody but you faulted me for. Old Woman! Are you there?"

He opened the screen and stepped inside. "You here? You all right? Old folks got no business living alone, away out at the back of beyond!"

He moved farther into the room, and she slipped up the porch and into the house. "I'm here, Amos. Right here, where I've been for forty years. Alone and without my sister, though that need not have been so."

She clicked her fingers softly behind her, and Rupe came to stand in the darkness beside the path of light. "So nobody ever faulted you for Rose, eh? Nobody ever thought about her after she was gone. She was quiet, my sister. Quiet and shy and afraid to say boo to a goose. Afraid to tell you about the baby. I made her tell you, in the end, though it did more harm than good."

Her voice took on an edge, and she struggled to control it.

"I knew you were rotten, the first time you came to take her to a camp meeting."

The man jerked around at her first word. He stared at her in the dim red light. "What baby? Don't think you can trick me, Old Woman. I don't know anything about no baby or about your precious Rose, either. I took her to preaching a few times, and riding once or twice. Nothing to make a fuss over...what are you doing?"

Ole Woman had taken a bit of paper from the pocket of her apron. She thrust it at him, taking care not to touch his fingers as he took it from her. "Read that. And then tell me you had nothing to do with Rose's death!"

He stared down, squinted hard, stretched his arms and turned to the lamp. As he read the scribbled note, he paled until the stubble of beard stood out dark against his bluish skin.

"Yes, she killed herself, but if you'd done right by her she would have had no need. You might as well have pushed her into the river yourself, and held her under until she drowned. She'd never have killed herself but for you."

He stared at her, his color slowly returning. "So? What can you do about it now? Nothing! Never could and never will. A scandal forty years old is nothing. You should have yelled long before now, if you wanted my hide."

She chuckled. "Been working for forty years to fix your comeuppance. Been studying on it and other things as well. Found out a heap of things nobody suspects exist, and fortune-telling's the least of the bunch. You just watch...."

She stepped aside, and Rupe came into the house, his ears back, his brown eyes turned green and frightful. A more fearsome looking creature you never could see, she reckoned. Amos moved back, but the dog herded him to the door, onto the porch, and when the man leaped down to run the dog paused as Amos stopped and gasped. A cougar stood in the dim moonlight, looking up the track of lamplight with eyes that glowed green to match the dog's.

Old Woman moved past the man to the dry well and heaved the heavy cover aside. The scent of bruised honeysuckle filled the night. "You know how long it takes to make a panther do your will?" she asked, though she never expected an answer. "Here!" she called. "Bring him here!"

The dog dropped behind, the cat moved cautiously at one side, as Amos sidled toward her, his face pale in the darkness, his breath coming harsh in his throat. He couldn't see the well, for all his attention was fixed on the cougar. When he came up beside the swing, he turned to face her.

Now Old Woman knew that her own eyes glowed green, blazing in the shadow of the tree to match those of her familiars. Amos gasped and glanced about, but he stood at the center of a triangle of stares, which moved forward, forcing him toward a square of deeper blackness, from which came an irritable sound, like corn shucks rustling.

Or rattlesnakes?

"What are you doing?" He made a desperate dart, but the cat herded him easily back into place.

Old Woman grinned, as she crooned, "Oh, what indeed? Been working and working for years, getting a handle on the beasts. Then I worked and worked for months, catching all them rattlers. And now it's ready, all ready, Amos, and you're about to pay up for forty years of living high and handsome, while my Rosie rots in her grave."

He tried to dash to the right again, but Rupe set his teeth into his calf and brought him to his knees. He struggled toward the left, but the cat lowered its face so close to him that he could smell the rank odor of its breath. He groaned as Old Woman reached down her hard brown arms, grabbed him, and gave a heave.

The groan turned into a scream, as he landed with a crunch amid a storm of rattles. There came a lot of shrieks, after that, and pleading wails as the cover went back onto the well. The honey-suckle was smoothed over again, leaving no trace that the thing had been opened.

Old Woman sat in the swing beside the well. The moon was down. The whip-poor-will had moved away into the woods, its cry now faint with distance. The frogs and crickets kept up their music, but a new note joined the song for a time.

Old Woman sat in the dark as long as that music lasted. When it ended, about midnight, she sighed and went into her cabin to bed.

Now she had her vengeance. But what would she do tomorrow?

My Dad was a traveling salesman, back in the days when the roads in East Texas were very long mud holes. Fortunately, he never ran into a problem like this….

THE CREEK, IT DONE RIZ

Only the Lord knows why I ever took the old road that day, particularly since the water was out all over the map from the big rains. I could have stuck a dozen times, coming across the bottom lands. It's a wonder in this world that none of the rickety little bridges were washed out—or that one of them didn't go out with me halfway across. Still, Pa's old 1939 Plymouth could mighty nearly swim, and we always took it out when we were going way down into the boondocks.

The whole thing was a lot of foolishness, anyway. I didn't get a degree from Texas A&M in order to go paddling around in the river-bottom in the middle of a flood to count hogs. But try telling the boss that. He sits in his air-conditioned office, thinking up dumb schemes, and never knows if it rains or shines. And he can come up with some of the gosh-awfulest ideas. A hog census! Now I ask you, how he thought that knowing where every hog in the county was located would help him sell his damn feed, I don't know.

Anyway, there I was in the river bottom in a car twice as old as I was, sloshing down a road that wasn't much more than a lane, when I could see it, which wasn't often. The wet sweetgum saplings were bent way down and slapping across the windshield. I was crawling along, cussing some, when I saw something out in the woods.

I crept on until I could feel gravel under the wheels; then I stopped. I could have sworn I saw an old man sitting on a stump. I stuck my feet into the rubber boots I had learned to take along with me, being as most hog-pens can't be said to do shoes any good at all. Then I got out and started off into a thicket. And sure enough, there was a grizzly-headed old cuss, soaked to the bone, dripping water off his nose and his eyebrows. He never acted as if he saw me, just muttered to himself as if that's what he'd been doing for quite a while.

When I got close enough to hear, I stood there for a minute, admiring his style. You don't hear cussing like that any more, with real feeling and meaning to it. And he was cussing the weather, which deserved everything he gave it and then some. But it was wet as all get-out, and finally I went up and touched him on the shoulder.

"Sir, I beg your pardon," I said, "but would you like a ride someplace? Out of the wet?"

He gave a jerk and looked up at me for a minute, sizing me up. Then he gave me a couple of cusses too.

I shook my head admiringly. "It's a privilege to listen to a man who can handle the language the way you do," I said. "Even my Pa, and he's no slouch, can't touch you. But it does look like you're set to catch your death of cold, if you sit out here much longer."

Then he squinched up his eyes and looked me over, real carefully. "You look to be a Jenkins," he said, when he had gone from top to bottom. "Got that Jenkins jaw. Any kin to Ralph Jenkins?"

"That's my Pa," I said. It's the darndest thing—anyplace I go, people spot me for Pa's son right off. Even if they never laid eyes on me before.

He grunted and shifted on the stump. "Tell you, Son," he said, "I ain't got no place to go that you can take me to in no car. But bein' as you're Ralph's boy, why, you might help me out a little bit."

Now that's where I should've said goodbye and been off to count hogs. But Pa raised us all to be polite and helpful to old folks, and I can't seem to break the habit. When an old geezer looks at you kind of slant-eyed, with his head cocked on one side like he's figuring out how far he can con you, it's time to take off. Not me, though. No brains, that's me.

So pretty soon I found myself slogging down a pig-trail through the woods, looking sharp for cotton-mouth moccasins and stump-holes. He kept talking all the time, as if he was scared I'd change my mind and leave him. Nothing he said made me anxious to keep on.

"I've got a kind of boat a little piece further on, tied up along Eel Creek. If it's still there, we can take it and get up to my house. The house ain't washed away; it's just the damn creek's done riz so I can't get to the yard. With a strong young fellow like you to help me with the boat, I kin make it." He paused and panted a while. I could see that he wasn't in too good shape.

I turned around and said, "Why, Pa could put you up until the water goes down. He'd be glad to. Why don't you just go back to the car with me, and I'll take you straight on in and have you dry in no time at all."

He started shaking his head before I was done. Then he looked all around, really careful, as if anybody but a couple of fools would have been out in the woods with the river out of its banks.

"I guess I ought to tell you, Son, seein' as how you're helpin' me and all. I've got my life's savings buried in that yard. If the river backs the creek up too high, it'll likely wash it right away. It's all I've got to stand me through my old age. I just got to get back there and get it out before the water comes up any more."

Well, he did sound pitiful. I couldn't help but wonder why he didn't dig up his money before he left, but I guessed that you might be forgetful at his age. So we went on, and the water was mighty near the tops of my boots before we came to his boat. Then I saw why he called it a kind of a boat. The baling bucket was the only thing that didn't have a hole in it. A good, sound log would have been a lot safer to try to travel on.

"You sure you want to risk that thing?" I asked him.

"It's a sight better than it looks," he answered. "I been fishing in that boat for twenty years and never drowned yet." I never was one to believe in miracles, but maybe such things happen, or else he was an uncommonly solid ghost. But I was pledged to help him, so I bailed out the water that was sloshing around in the bottom of the thing and heaved it out into the creek. I stood there and watched the little wiggles of water come through the holes and start moving down the sides.

He got right in and started bailing. "Reason I had to have help," he said, "is somebody has to bail while the other one rows. I always borrow one of Rupe Miller's kids to do the bailing, when I go fishing, but they left when the water got high. Get in, Boy. Let's get moving. That water's not going to wait on us."

So I said a prayer, which would have pleased Ma, and got in. Then I didn't have time to pray. That water was wild as a yearling colt. It took everything I could do to keep the boat from taking off in ten directions at once.

I fought with the paddle to fend us off floating logs and brush-piles. I guess I came nearer to poling it along than paddling. In the middle of all that, it came to me...I didn't know his name. I twisted my head round and yelled, "Hey, Mister, what's your name?"

He looked up from his bucket, kind of startled. "Why, I'm Abe Willitts. I thought everybody in the county knowed of old Abe."

Then I really started to sweat. Everybody knew about Abe Willitts, sure enough. When I was little, Ma'd hush me up with, "Crazy Abe'll get you, if you don't be good." When his wife died, all the women looked at each other and said, "He finally killed her. I knew he would one day." And nobody could prove them wrong, because she was buried by the time he got around to letting anybody know she was dead.

Even Pa, who wouldn't hear a bad word about anyone, had to be still when that hunter disappeared. He'd told his wife that he was going to bird-hunt down in the bottoms, and he'd intended to get Abe and his setter to help him find the birds. Nobody ever saw nor heard from him again. They looked too. All over the place, with dogs and men. Abe claimed he never got there at all, and nobody could prove different.

So here I was in a leaky boat in the middle of a flood with a crazy man. A hog census looked mighty calm and peaceful, when I thought about it. Still, I hadn't time to worry overmuch just then. Working that crazy piece of junk around the bends in the creek took all my energy. By the time we came in sight of the house, I was done in, sure enough.

Abe jumped out onto the bank, only it was the yard fence, the bank being a hundred yards behind us in the middle of the flood, and tied his rope to a fencepost. "Here we are, Boy. You just wait right here, and I'll go round and dig up my savings and be right back." His eyes slid round at me and didn't look quite sane.

"I'm too tired to move, Sir," I said. "You just get your stuff, and I'll rest. It'll take all we both can do to get us back up that creek."

Soon as he was gone around the house, I slid out of the boat and eased up the slope. It took a while, and once he looked out around the corner of the porch to see if I was still in the boat. Luckily, I'd propped up the bucket so it looked like a head leaning against the edge, and he didn't go down to check. I stayed hidden in the bushes for a while to let my heart quit thumping, then I went on.

When I peeped around the porch, he was digging hard. You could hear his shovel going "Shloop! Shloop!" in the mud, because the water had got around to that side of the house too. He was in an almighty hurry. I scootched down and watched. I don't quite know why, but I just had to know what it was he was in such a hurry and a sweat about. He had to be living on Social Security, just like Pa and everybody else their age. I figured he couldn't have saved up enough to amount to anything.

When a shovelful of mud came out of that hole with something dark and solid on it, I perked up. It was a hunting jacket, as I could tell after it lay there a while and the rain washed off the mud. The kind with a bag in back for shot birds and shell-pockets across the front. Then Abe's hand came up with a shotgun in it and laid it on the ground.

I didn't wait to see more. All of a sudden, I figured I'd better be back at the boat—or further still—when Abe came around the corner of that house. I made it a lot quicker than I'd come and leaned back in the boat as if I'd been dozing. Then I got to thinking.

Whatever he was getting out of that hole, he'd likely send down the flood. Maybe he'd feel safe then. Maybe not.... The more I thought about going back up that creek with him bailing behind me, the less I liked the notion. I had a little money in my pocket. Probably about what that hunter had had. And nobody knew where I was or what I was doing.

I eased out into the bushes and crept along until I found a likely log. It was half afloat, already, so I goosed it out into the current and held onto a stub of branch, with my head close under the side so it couldn't be seen. That log and I whirled and twirled and twiddled down the creek with the rest of the stuff floating there until we lodged way down on Bobcat Ridge. I guess Abe never did know what happened to me.

He must've tried to make it back in that boat, all by himself. We'll never know, though. They didn't look for him nearly as hard as they did for that hunter.

Every kind of misdeed can be found in the East Texas woods, from murder to burglary, but it is only in the past couple of decades that deep woods people have begun locking their doors. However—it is not a good idea to be caught inside somebody else's house without a darn good reason.

ON THE STUMPS

I never expected Stanbridge to be at home. On a bright, late-spring day down there in the river bottom country, he should've been out in his boat, setting lines or running nets or just lazing along with a cane pole in his hand and his hat over his eyes, letting the boat drift with the current. I'd like to have been doing that myself.

But I'm a poor man. Have to keep plugging along, without any time taken off for playing around. Anybody who thinks thieving is easy work just never tried it. I have spent more time hiding in closets or under beds—even down a well, once—than you would ever believe. People do tend to come home at the damndest times!

But Eph Stanbridge was steady as a clock. I'd watched him for two weeks, and every decent morning (and even a few that weren't fit for man or beast) he was off down the river in that blue boat of his. He never came home until late in the evening, and sometimes it was full dark when he got there. I'd be all mosquito-bit, lying up in the woods watching for him.

I'd done my homework carefully. There wasn't a reason in the world why the job shouldn't have gone off slick as a whistle.

Eph lived so far at the back of beyond that he never worried about visitors even, much less burglars. He hadn't any window blinds, being as there was nothing out there in the woods to look in at him at night but skunks or bobcats or water moccasins. It was easy for me to creep up to the window and watch him potter around the house. I knew that if I watched him for long enough, finally I'd see where he hid his money.

And sure enough I did. It took ten days, and I was swollen up all over with chigger and mosquito bites. But he made a trip to town to sell his catfish to the café, and when he got home he went straight to the mantel over his fireplace. I could see plainly the way he reached down and pulled on the side piece over to the left, and it opened out just like a little door. He put a roll of bills into a wooden box.

I couldn't see what else was in the box, because of the angle, but I was willing to bet there were a lot more rolls of bills that had been dropped into that box over the years. Eph never spent a dime for anything but flour, sugar, coffee, and chewing tobacco.

I picked a day so warm and sun-bright that you could have spread it like honey on toast. Nobody could stay home on a day like that unless he was sick enough to die. And sure enough, there was nobody in the house when I got there. His boat was gone too, along with the coils of trotline he kept on his little pier. Nothing ever looked safer. Mind you, I wasn't careless. I went off down the Reed Slough road to the end and left my car there as if I'd gone fishing in a boat. Cut through the woods across the big flat in the river's bend until I caught the track that runs alongside the water for miles. That took me right around behind Eph's hog pen. His house was right up the twisty path, and I cut behind it, through the peach orchard and garden, and crept up to the back door.

The house was as still as a big gray animal dozing in the sun. There wasn't a speck of smoke left in the air, and I knew he'd cooked his breakfast long ago. The wood stove was cool.

Still, I didn't rush it. I went up on the back porch and called him, real loud. "Eph! You at home?" I had brought a length of trot-line I could claim I'd found fastened to a floating log, and my excuse for being there would have been that I thought it might be his.

He might have thought it was peculiar, as such things are usually finders' keepers, but Eph was so easygoing he'd have accepted that. But there wasn't any answer but a sort of echo through the empty rooms. The screen door was open. Nobody down in the river bottoms ever locks his door. Only the summer people in the lake houses downriver have to worry about being robbed—nobody else has anything much to steal.

I pushed open the door; it screeched like a banshee. Nearly scared me out of my boots. The house was just about what you'd expect of an old bachelor. Plain as to furnishings, dusty as to tables and floors, but tidy too. He liked things in their own places, I could see. I liked that in a man.

I went through the kitchen and up the wide hall down the middle of the house. The parlor where the hidey-hole was opened off to the right. The floor creaked and complained, no matter how lightly I tried to step, but there was nobody there to hear. It's just that unnecessary noise makes any thief nervous.

The parlor still held traces of Eph's wife. There was a red plush sofa that was about twice as old as I was. The oil lamp hanging from a hook over the middle of that table was a pretty thing. I'd seen the like in catalogs—they call them Tiffany style, and this one had to be the real thing. But I hadn't time to look around.

Once you knew where to look, it wasn't hard to find that mantel-door. The ten-inch pine plank that formed the surround had a notch cut into its back edge, easy to feel when you ran a finger down the cranny. I pulled it, and the thing swung out. It didn't even squeak.

I did.

Four snakes came rippling out into the room. Two of them nailed me before I could jump. Right through my leather lace-up boots. One was a diamond-back rattler that had to be six feet long. One was an ugly old moccasin the color of ash. The other two got away among the furniture before I could identify them, but I think one was a copperhead. Damn!

I sat on the floor and took off the boots, though my legs were already swollen enough to make it a bad job. I split my pants legs so I could get to the bites—that was one big sucker of a rattler. There was an inch-wide gap between the fang marks.

Tears were rolling down my face, and my heart was thumping away like a steam engine, trying to circulate that poison even faster. I knew I had to get it out, right now. I fumbled my pocket knife out and set the blade on the marks on my left leg. It was sharp, and a drop of blood beaded away as I closed my eyes and pushed the blade into my skin.

My God!

Without taking time to think, I cut again, across the first slash. The other leg got tended to before I had time to begin feeling the first one too bad. Then I was busy squeezing the poison out—anybody who tries to suck it is a fool.

But I could feel it burning up the veins of my shins. You never get it all out, and with two snakes—different kinds at that!—there was just no way the easy method was going to work. I had to do something mighty fast, or Eph would come home to find a bloated corpse in his parlor.

I'd seen a hacksaw in the hall, hanging on a hook with other tools. I crawled out and found it in the dimness. I didn't need light for what I had to do; it was better not to see.

I set the blade against my hairy shin, about six inches above the bite, and shivered for a minute before getting up the nerve to begin. But the burn was moving upward, and I knew I had to do it now. I bore down and sawed across my leg down into the flesh.

Used to be that I'd trap for animals in the woods and around the creeks to earn school money. Many's the time I've found a furry paw in a trap, and the rest of the beast would be long gone. I never thought how it would feel to chew off your own foot to go free.

Now I knew.

All my nerves were jangling so that my hands could hardly grip the saw. I shook like a willow in the wind, and when I hit the bone, that first time, I thought I was going to come to pieces, right there and then. You take all the worst sensations of a dentist's drill going into a nerve and add it to the feeling of a broken bone, and that's how it felt, only worse.

I don't know how I got through that first leg bone. The second was just sort of done by instinct, being as I was still in shock from the first. By the time both my lower legs were lying in puddles of blood on the pine planking of the floor, I was crying like a kid. I tied off both stumps with my galluses, but there was still a lot of blood, and I had to keep tightening those tourniquets to keep from bleeding to death then and there.

When I finally pulled myself together and began thinking, I knew there was no way to get out of this clean. Even if I shut the mantel-door, Eph would know the minute he walked in the house that something terrible had happened, and he'd miss his snakes as soon as he looked in the hidey-hole.

The money was still in place, of course, but he wasn't going to be pleased. No matter how easygoing, nobody wants anyone pilfering around in his house, not to mention messing up his floor.

I wondered if there was a way I could crawl off through the woods. I was getting pretty weak; still, I thought I'd give it a try, but I'd have to take the legs with me. I can't think of a better way to identify a man than by his own legs. I tied them together with the trotline in my pocket, and then I set out crawling toward the kitchen, though I thought every time I moved that I would faint.

But I almost died of shock when I scootched through the door. First thing I saw was two big feet in rubber boots under the kitchen table. I looked farther up, and there was Eph, smiling. I didn't take that grin to be an easygoing one, either. His eyes were round and blue as china plates, and he looked like a cheerful old grampa, but I had a feeling he wasn't one bit happy.

"I knew you'd make it today," he said. "Been feeling you

watching me for a couple of weeks, now. Funny...you can't fool a man who lives in the woods and on the water. And the fellows were so uneasy, I knew you'd probably come today."

"The fellows?" My voice sounded choked, even to me.

"My friends who live in the wall. Jesse and Arthur and Percy and Steven. You let 'em out and they ran off, but they'll be home again. Back in their nice dark place behind the fireplace. It's remarkable how snakes like to live close to a fireplace; they keep lively all winter. Lots of company for an old man by himself."

I never had any fellow feeling for a man who liked snakes. There was always something strange about them. Something that made my skin crawl.

I groaned and put my head into my hands for a minute. Then I looked up and asked, "You sending for the sheriff?"

"Whyever for?" His voice was smooth as cream.

"For coming into your house and trying to rob you."

He laughed. "I took out all the money as soon as I knew somebody was watching me. There wasn't a thing in my hidey-hole except the boys."

I looked at my stumps, swollen like elephant legs at the ends of the trotline. Tears rolled down my face again. All this suffering, permanent crippling, for nothing at all! My stumps were throbbing now, and the poison that had got through to the rest of me was making me sick and groggy. My feet itched fiercely.

"But you'll have me put away! I'll go to jail," I wailed.

"Now why should I do that?" The voice was cream with honey, now. "You didn't steal anything. Just let out my pets, but they always come back. Anybody is welcome in my house—there's nothing wrong with that. Besides, you're never going to steal anything again. Are you?" Those blue eyes were stabbing right through me.

I looked away, down at my bloody stumps. A legless thief—no, it didn't look as if I ever would steal again.

I shook my head.

He poured a slug of white lightning down me to kill some of the pain. Then he lugged me out to his ancient pickup and took me to town to the hospital. He told the sheriff that I'd been snake-bit and cut off my legs to save my life, which was the Gospel truth. Said nothing at all about why I'd been out there. I agreed with everything, though by then I was mighty sick from the poison that got up into my system while I was sawing off my legs.

So that's what happened to my legs. That's why I sell pencils on the street corner. Nice of you to ask. Not many do, these days. Everybody in town has heard the story by now. It's only when visitors like you come that I get to tell it again.

There's the five o'clock whistle at the sawmill. Time to go back to my room. Why, thank you. Not everybody helps me gather up my stuff onto my cart. Neat job, isn't it? I push it along with my crutches...see?

Eph made it for me. He keeps an eye on me and comes to see me whenever he gets to town. Brings me fresh catfish too. I have the feeling that if I even so much as shortchange anybody, those round blue eyes will see it.

Eph's a good old man. Just don't ever try to rob him.

Living out here in the woods, I used to lie in bed at night and listen to the coon hounds belling through the distant forest. I never wanted to follow them, but I did enjoy listening. Coon hunters find a lot of things, though maybe not so oddball as this one did.

COON HUNT, WITH DISTRACTIONS

The hound gave a yip and took off through the moonlight. I sighed and sat under a hollow sweetgum tree and listened to Old Rupe go hollering through the thickets. That was no way to coon-hunt, really, but I had nobody to go with. There wasn't even another dog to run with Rupe.

But the fall nights were just too fine to spend indoors, no matter what Becky-Sue thought about it. Women just do not understand coon hunting.

Rupe was a fine dog, old of course, but that just meant he made up in smart what he lacked in stamina. He might not be able to run clean out of the county and keep up with a young pack anymore, but let him tangle with a big old boar coon and you'd see the fur fly.

I could hear him, his voice belling clean and sure, as he trailed. The hills flow low and rounded between the river and the new freeway off to the west of my little farm, and sound carries for miles, the way the woods lie. I'd be able to hear when he treed the coon, and I was feeling just vinegary enough to go and smoke the animal out, if it took me all night. The moon was full, and I felt fit for anything.

Almost anything.

It was coming up on midnight when Rupe's voice changed. Instead of the regular "Here I am and I'm going this way" peals, he sounded shrill. Almost frightened. Now his voice was telling me to come quick—he had hold of something he couldn't figure out what to do with.

I stood and shook the stiffness out, and then I headed toward the river. Rupe was still yelling for me to come, and all my years of school teaching hadn't made me as slow as you would think. I did a lot of hunting and fishing. It made Becky-Sue furious, but I'd left teaching because I refused to spend my weekends in a suit and tie, toadying to trustees.

That was why I left the job and came back to the farm. It took Becky-Sue six months to decide that she'd rather come with me than stay there in town all by herself teaching. She'd never admit it, but she'd had a bellyful of teaching too. She's no idiot, and that seems to be what they want nowadays.

Now I was running through the woods as if I was still twenty-five, instead of a good ten years older. I did my best, though, and the faster I ran, the harder Rupe yelled. I hightailed it down the animal tracks and through the thickets as if it was a jogging trail, which it wasn't. Not by a long shot.

I hadn't a gun—never carried one on my coon hunts—and as I ran I wondered if he'd found a big old granddaddy coon that was too big and smart for him to handle. I kept watch for a stout hickory sapling, because I knew there was no way I could lick one if Rupe couldn't. Getting mauled by a coon is no joke—they can tear you to flinders. Not to mention what they can do to a dog.

I cut through a pine thicket toward the sound of Rupe's voice. Just beyond it was a tangle of huckleberry, and I got hung up in that, which slowed me down. By then Rupe was whimpering and yelping and crying and yipping by turns. I couldn't figure out what in tunket he had got himself involved with. If it had been a skunk, I'd have smelled it by now, I was sure, because I was getting pretty close.

I left part of my sweater and a good chunk of my religion in the bushes, but at last I was out and found a good clear trail that somebody's cows used to go down to the river to drink. Right ahead was Rupe, and he made enough noise for a whole pack of coon hounds.

I slowed to a walk and went softly the last few yards. My Dad saw the last bear that was in these woods, I thought, but I didn't want to take a chance that they'd made a comeback. And then I smelled something.

You take rotten. That can be nasty. Skunk is awful, but it's a clean smell, sort of, like burnt coffee. Spoiled canned goods can turn your stomach. Put all those stinks together, and add a pinch of something that made your hackles rise, and you'd have the stink I was smelling. I was too far under the cover of the woods for the moon to do much good. My hand-generated flash was in my sweater pocket, and I dug it out and began pumping the handle. That bluish light pulsed into the black shadows, making the dust of the path shine like snow.

Rupe was a dark blot on that pale track. I swept the flickering beam up the path, toward the spot where Rupe was staring. It touched a dark bulk that was no bush.

That thing was BIG. Not even a bear would have been that size. A pair of eyes glinted red in the light as I stood, stunned. Then the thing turned and took off up the path, ambling along as if it wasn't a bit afraid of me. That was when I saw that it wasn't nearly as hairy as a bear. Patches of skin showed between taggles of scroungy fur.

It's a good thing it left, for I couldn't stir. I stood there for several minutes, squeezing the flash to keep from being in the dark, but I wasn't able to stir a foot. Rupe brought me to when he started shivering against my leg. He had more sense than to chase anything like that.

He licked my hand, and that did it. Rupe whimpered and looked off into the brush. Then he looked at me again, into the brush again, and when he looked at me once more, I could see impatience in his eyes.

I wasn't really anxious to find anything else that night, and I certainly didn't want anything to find me. But I knew Rupe. He knew something was in that patch of sawvines, and he wouldn't quit fussing until I found what it was.

I refused to go into any brush patch armed with a flashlight. I hunted around and found that sapling I needed, broke the top off across my knee, and then, armed with a very iffy weapon, I started into the dark tangle of stickers and brush.

First there was the glint of metal under my light. It resolved itself into a gun barrel—a curved gun barrel. There was a whitish blur behind it, and when I turned my light on it the most godawful face I ever saw stared back at me from dead eyes. I'll have nightmares about that forever.

There was worse. That face was split half in two, down the middle. I looked at the gun barrel. That had done the job, and it was very, very messy. Whoever had used it had twisted that gun into a pretzel and flung it down beside his victim and left. Or had he? I remembered the size of the creature I had met on the path.

I backed out of the patch, my shoulder blades feeling a cold spot right in the middle. I shook all over, thinking of what might come back down that trail and be waiting for me. But the path was clear, except for the dark dabs of cow manure.

Rupe was shaking so hard against my legs that I had a hard time standing. It felt as if a hundred miles lay between me and any human help. The slim pulse of light from my flash didn't comfort me at all.

When I was a boy, I knew that country like my own barnyard. Things had changed a lot since I was a boy: farms had been sold and resold; families had moved away and left empty houses and fields lying fallow. There was a house, I knew, toward the freeway, but that would have meant going in the same direction as that Whatever. No way!

My home was five miles or so to the south, and I didn't want to go flying through those thickets again. My best chance was to follow the river downstream, for there was a big automated dairy there. It would have a phone and probably a crew with a man in charge. I hoped he owned a shotgun.

It was almost as light as day, once I reached the path along the river. The moon was just past the zenith, and the rocks in the streambed sparkled amid a glimmer of ripples. I felt better there, and Rupe did too. We went down faster than I'd have dared in full summer, when the water moccasins were out. We fairly flew along.

After a bit, something that had been nagging me worked up to the top of my mind. The air held a taint of that smell I'd found on the path in the woods. It was growing steadily stronger. I stopped for a minute, and there came a rustle in the woods. It halted almost as quickly as I did. I moved again and stepped to clear a muddy patch in the trail. Then I froze.

At the edge of the mud, etched clearly in shadow by the moonlight, was a footprint. Half again as big as mine, bare, with a strange sort of mark where the toes had gripped the ground like fingers. A gorilla, I thought, might make a mark like that.

There was another sound, and my heart raced for a moment. Then I relaxed, for it was my own breath, whistling in my throat. I forced myself to settle down. We were being tracked, off in the woods, by one or more of the things I had seen. Rupe knew it too. He was snarling so deep in his throat that it was almost inaudible.

I had no weapon but the sapling. I was trapped against the river, for I felt certain the thing could swim faster than I could; I could think of only one move to make. I had to go on downstream, fast enough to keep ahead, not so fast the things would begin chasing me.

Then I looked down at Rupe. I've said he was smart, but that leaves a lot unstated. He was well-nigh human when it came to understanding. On the days when Becky-Sue got up on the wrong side of the bed, he was a model dog, and I took my cue from him. For days before I knew it myself, he knew when I was going hunting.

I could tell him anything reasonable, and if he felt like doing it, he would. But this was going to be the most complicated thing I had ever tried to get across to him.

I waited until we hit a wide patch of beach, curving out into a bend of the stream. I followed it out until we were a good thirty yards from the edge of the trees. Then I paused and knelt, fiddling with a bootlace, while I said to the hound, "Go downriver, Rupe. Go find a man. Find a man, boy! Bring him!"

I was going to be right behind him, if I was let. I figured the critters would let him go—he wasn't as big as I was and he was a hell of a lot faster. His scraggly tail waved back and forth; his tongue lolloped out in a quick grin, and he was gone.

Once he was out of sight, I felt lonelier than I ever had before in my life. Now there was nothing but me and the thing—or things—in the woods. Even Rupe's shivering against my knee had reassured me that there was one thing in the world more scared than I was.

I moved onward, my pace deliberate. When I hurried, my un-seen companion edged closer through the underbrush, the deep whoosh of its breath audible. When I went too slowly, I could see the brush rippling as it pushed through, and that didn't comfort me a bit.

It seemed like hours that we went down the path, the moon seeming to be glued in the same spot in the sky. Time seemed not to be passing as fast for that moon as it was for me. Then, far ahead, I heard a sound—a dog's high-pitched bark. Rupe. The blast of a shotgun followed on the heels of that cry, and I could hear a hubbub. I lit out running as hard as I could, forgetting the stalker in the woods.

That thing was *fast*! It was after me instantly, but sheer panic gave me more speed than ever before. I stayed ahead of it around two bends. Then I saw light ahead—the glare of lanterns and the white flare of flashlights. A speeding shape bulleted into me, knock-ing me flat just in time for a load of buckshot to zing over me.

There was a startled grunt, off in the brush, and I rolled clear of the path to let a mess of snarling Dobermans go tearing past. There was a terrific crashing and growling in the woods, and I figured that those devils would take the thing down, if anything could.

Then there was a shriek you wouldn't believe could come out of a dog, and the whole pack went screaming back the way they came. They almost ran down the burly fellow leading the men with the lights and guns.

"What in the blue-toe-nailed hell is going on?" he yelled.

I rose up almost under his feet, with old Rupe tying himself in knots around my legs. "That thing's been following us through the woods. Your dogs tangled with it. There's a dead man upriver, if I can find him again, and if I can't, Rupe can. I saw what killed him, I think. That thing, or one just like it." I shivered hard.

The men had gathered around me, now, their faces grim.

"There it stood in the middle of the path," I said, "seven feet tall if it was an inch. Face on it like nothing you ever saw, hair all over with skin showing through. It walked away as if I wasn't worth bothering with. And then Rupe showed me the corpse. Its head was split open with its own gun.

"The thing followed us, and I sent Rupe ahead to get help." I was chattering too much, and my teeth were beginning to join in, but the big man put his hand on my shoulder.

"Damndest dog I ever did see," he said. "We were getting ready to go to bed, when that hound ran against the door like he was going to bust right in. Gage looked out and give him a cussing and let off a round of shot, but that didn't faze him. He set in the yard and raised Cain till I got the gun and went out to shoot him. He come right up to me and grabbed my pants leg and tried to haul me off upriver.

"I don't claim to be awful bright, but I know a good dog when I see it, and this 'un was telling me something just as plain as he could, so I called out the crew and turned the dogs loose, and here we come. But what in tarnation could scare those devils?"

"Believe me, you don't want to find out. Just come with me and help me find that body. I don't know if the thing will come back and eat it or bury it or haul it off, but we might hurry, just the same."

The trip upriver was far more cheerful than the one down had been. Hal Bartley, the big foreman of the dairy, knew that river like the fisherman he was. He knew just the cow trail that ran down to the water. And once we found that, the rest was only very messy details.

I got home with the dawn. Becky-Sue was in the kitchen, listening to the coffeepot bubbling and thinking up mean things to say to me when I came up the path through the back yard. But I fooled her. The foreman sent me home in a pickup, and Gage let me off at my front gate.

I staggered up the flagged walk, followed by Rupe, who was even more beat than I was. I let the front screen bang shut, and Becky-Sue was out of the kitchen and up the hall in half a shake, her checkered shirt-tail popping in the breeze.

She halted in the door, her gaze going from Rupe to me and back again. "What happened to you two?" she asked.

I told her, while she dished up bacon and flapjacks and Rupe gobbled a bowl of oatmeal (his favorite dish).

"You mean to tell me that there is a monster like that wandering down there in the woods?" she asked.

"More than one, I think. Two, I feel sure, stalked us down the river path."

"And who was the dead man?" She was busy wiping down the stovetop.

"Bartley knew him. He was part-time help at the dairy, and he'd gone squirrel hunting. His gun had been fired, but squirrel shot couldn't possibly have stopped that thing. He would have been better off if he'd been like me—with not even a stick that *looked* like a gun. I suspect those things have gotten wary of firearms, if they've met many hunters in the woods."

I finished my coffee and looked up at her. "I've just about lost my taste for coon hunting. When Rupe and I get an itch to run in the woods, we're going to do it in the daytime. And not downriver. Okay?"

She grinned. "In one month, you'll both be down there hunting that whachmacallit," she said. There wasn't a trace of doubt in her tone. "I've already seen you cutting your eyes around toward the gun rack, wondering if the .306 will stop it. If you score the slugs across the ends of the lead to make them spread on impact, they just might. But those things have a right to live too, Bruce Williams. You think about that, before you go hunting them."

I looked down at my plate. Becky-Sue may not appreciate coon hunting, but she has me down cold. She was right. I was already thinking about going after the thing that had scared me so.

I listened close to the radio and the TV news for a few days, while the sheriff's men combed the woods around the spot where the body was found. They came up with some mighty strange tracks, but that was all.

They also came and questioned me more than once, but anybody looking at what was done to that gun, not to mention the skull of the dead man, could see that a middle-aged ex-schoolteacher simply couldn't have done either one, even if he'd had a motive, which I hadn't.

After a while things calmed down and no more investigators roamed around in the woods. That was when I took Becky-Sue's advice and scored some rounds across the ends of the slugs and set off with Rupe again.

By now the moon was dark, and I took with me a big hand light we used around the farm. It weighed a ton, but it was mighty bright and the battery lasted for a lot of hours without running out of juice.

This wood wasn't the clean place I knew back when I was a boy. Once I got off our land and into the cut-over forest, it was a mad tangle of vines and saplings; dead tops left by loggers were grown up with persimmon sprouts, and it held hidden traps where the log trucks got stuck, winched out, and left deep holes that later weeds and brush grew over and covered up.

I could have gone the way I went before, of course, but I reckoned that the critter I'd seen wasn't going to be within miles of all the activity there had been there. I put myself in his place and decided I would be up in the logging company plantation, which was well grown but not ready to cut. It was the nearest good cover for miles.

I talked it over with Rupe, and while he looked pretty doubtful when I got through to him what I wanted, he set off, his tail low and his ears looking droopy. I followed him. Animals know things that people have forgotten, and he went pretty straight toward the place I'd picked.

I didn't go in the dark, did I mention that? I might be out after sundown, which is why I took the light, but I wasn't such a fool that I'd hunt one of those monsters by night. No, I intended to check out tracks and trails for footprints, and once I located those I had my plans pretty well made.

Rupe was a master hand at finding what he looked for, and before full dark he'd sniffed out a deer trail and started giving his "Here it is, why don't you come ahead and look at it?" yelp.

There were those oversized prints, all right: two sets, one smaller than the other. There was even the barest hint of overpowering stink left on the bushes alongside the trail. We were in the right place, and it was just on the edge of getting very dark indeed.

I cast around to find one of the big hardwoods they sometimes left among the pines, and sure enough there was a hickory tree at the fence line, its heavy branches black against the last light in the sky and bending over the path where the tracks appeared. I hitched my rifle around my shoulder, tucked the torch in my pack, and went up it, groaning all the way. The climbing you do so easily at ten is a lot harder in middle age, believe me.

Then I waited. Rupe was settled into a clump of huckleberry off to one side of the path, and I knew he'd let me know the minute anything walked up the trail, so I let myself rest, even doze a bit, once I had the spotlight hitched to a branch above my head and the rifle laid along the limb on which I was sitting, my back to the heavy trunk of the tree.

I woke when my head nodded forward. The pines rustled in a light breeze, but otherwise the night was quiet. An owl, way over toward the creek, gave a quavering cry, and a killdeer whimpered sadly as it flew. Then Rupe gave a growl, just barely loud enough for me to hear. I sat and hefted the rifle. My left hand was on the button of the light, and when Rupe gave his "Here they come!" bark, I pushed it down and looked along the path.

They were almost just below me, staring up toward the brilliant light as if it blinded them, freezing them in place. I had the rifle at my shoulder before I realized what I was seeing.

The big one was ugly, true, but those eyes, shining like a dog's in the beam, seemed somehow puzzled and anxious. Its arm was around the shoulders of the smaller one, and I took a good look at it, too. Damn! It was just a kid, its hair almost downy compared to that of its...father? Those eyes shone silver, and the awkward shape shrank against the other's side as if for protection.

All of a sudden it hit me. We humans had cut out the woods for miles all around the river. Who knows how many centuries these creatures had lived in the deep thickets, never being forced out where people would see them or pose a danger to them? And now that we had pushed them out of their natural place, we wanted to shoot them.

That man they killed over by the river had been, I was willing to bet, aiming to shoot the one that wrapped his gun around his head. Self-defense has always seemed to me to be the only rational reason for killing anything, now that we don't have to hunt for food. By that measure Old Ugly there had been perfectly justified in what he'd done.

I looked down at the gun in my hands. They weren't any danger for me. I sure as hell didn't want to eat them. Why was I here in a tree like some sort of silly owl, intending to kill something that belonged here far more than I did?

I clicked off the light. Rupe gave an inquiring snuffle, but I didn't hear anything at all. I gave them five minutes to move before I lit the torch again. The path was empty except for Rupe, who was looking disgusted and staring up at me, his eyes red in the beam.

I stayed in that tree all night. I wasn't any threat to the Whachmacallits any longer, but they didn't know that, and I did have a gun. It was obvious that they knew what guns could do, and I didn't want any accidents like the one that had killed that dairy hand.

When first light touched the treetops to the east, I went down, stiff and sore, and wondering what sort of madness had put me up there in the first place. Rupe came out of his nest in the bushes and wagged alongside as I headed for home.

I wondered what Becky-Sue would say when we came home with our story. Then I grinned into the dark woods of my own place, which were uncut, except for carefully chosen firewood, for generations. They might visit me here, sometime, wanting real forest instead of cutover crap.

Whistling, I went toward the lane leading home, Rupe dancing along ahead of me as if he was a young dog again. We both felt better, I think, than we had for days.

Becky-Sue would be proud of us.

Good fences make good neighbors, Robert Frost said. Fence lines sometimes cause murders in East Texas, because land is a sacred thing to us. The first person I ever knew who was murdered died over a disputed fence line.

KILLIN' FENCE

The fence glinted in the staring sunlight, its barbs tipped with savage points of light. It was a tight fence, as taut-strung as the men who stood, one on either side, staring across it.

"Three feet," said the tall man. "Three feet of my land. It'll come out of your hide, Sam, before I have done."

Sam shifted his weight uneasily, tucking a thumb in his worn leather belt. "Aw, Vince, come on! I split the difference, good as I could. What can you do when two surveyors say two different things? I just went halfway between 'em. If you'd been well enough to help build it, you'd have done the same thing, and no hard feelin's."

The taller man grunted, frowning in the shadow of his sweaty felt hat. "Bud Pearcy says different. He told me you moved the stakes yourself. Told me what you said too—so don't try to talk so sweet and reasonable."

"If you'll listen to Bud Pearcy now, you must've been sicker than I knew or you let on," interrupted Sam. "That greasy little snake'll make trouble just for fun, and you know it. Never was any feudin' around here, neighbor or family, that that squirt wasn't nosin' around in. Vince, we've been neighbors for twenty-two years right here, and never had any trouble at all until now. You've come to me when you needed somethin', and I've come to you. Are you goin' to let Bud put a spoke in both our wheels—over three feet of land that might be yours, but might just as well be mine?"

But Vince squinted his pale eyes and laid his hand on the top strand of wire. The sparks of light danced on the barbs as he shook it.

"Be damned to you. Be damned to your lies," he said, and he turned and walked into the woods-path behind him.

Sam shook his head as he watched his old friend go. Slowly, he pulled on his warped leather-palmed gloves, wiped his forehead on his sleeve and climbed back onto the tractor.

He was a puzzled man. Because of a man he thought of as "po' white trash," here he was about to get good and mad at a man for whom he had great respect.

I was sure I was doin' Vince a good turn, he thought. I bought all the wire and cut the posts off my own place and put up that fence to stay a while, without askin' him for anything, just because he had so much trouble with his heart and I felt like he could use the help. Didn't even ask him to buy staples. Why I let that sneakin' Bud help build it, I don't know.

He coughed in the dust raised by the hay rake.

Why the old-timey surveyors used trees for line markers, I don't understand, he mused. Didn't they know the trees would die, one day, and leave all sorts of stumps and root-holes that might be the one and might not? When Vince decided we needed a new line fence, I tried to get him to stick to the old line, but some college-kid county agent talked him into havin' the whole thing surveyed again. Pure D waste. And then the idiot of a surveyor couldn't take the old stump for a mark. Nossir, had to go and decide the old survey had used the wrong stump for a marker forty years ago.

I just couldn't see takin' six whole feet of land off Vince's place, even if it was his own doin'. So I did the best I could. Would've been fine, too, if old Bud hadn't come mooching around, crying for work.

The long line of dust swept behind him, round and round the field, as he combed the tangled hay into neat rows for the automatic baler. The sun basted the field with a sear of haze and shimmer, and the crickets zipped off in a brittle spray before the tractor. Sam jounced easily in the seat, his corded wrists and heavy shoulders running with sweat which, combined with the breeze of moving, kept him reasonably cool. But when Bud Pearcy stepped from the woods at the far edge of the field and waved for him to stop, he began to warm up in the region of his collar.

"What you want, Pearcy?" he demanded, cutting the throttle so he could hear the dirty little man when he spoke.

"Well, Sam, I reckoned I ought to come and tell you—warn you, like. Seems you really got Vince riled about that fence. He's plumb unreasonable. I come by his house—Mrs. Vince promised my woman some dresses she'd done with—and Vince come in, all hot and bothered, swearin' that for two cents he'd shoot you. I tried my best to smooth him out, and his wife, she done her best to calm him down, but the more I talked, the madder he got. So I reckoned I better run over here and let you know, so's you can steer clear of him until he cools off some. You're too smart to let name-callin' and cussin' and carryin' on like that get you down.

"I told Vince, I said, 'Sam Bullard's not the man to make trouble. He'll see things reasonable, if anybody will. You just go and talk things over with him, quiet like, and I'll bet you'll be friends again, right off'."

"But he got to ravin' about how you was always comin' after him to help load cattle or get in the hay when it looked like rain, and how seldom he ever called on you, and that it seemed to him he'd been livin' for twenty years right next to a bum and just now come to see it."

"Course, Mrs. Vince, she reminded him of all the times you got up out of bed to drive him to the hospital, when he'd have those heart spells, but seemed like he didn't remember at all. It's real funny," and the little man heaved a greasy sigh, "how bein' sick will change a man and make him so ungrateful and forgetful."

Sam had listened silently, but his neck grew redder and his face was mottled with dark patches of blood, under his fair skin.

"Bud," he said in a mild tone, "You'd better get your tail off this place and don't ever come back, even if all your brats take scarlet fever at once and your house is on fire to boot. I don't like the looks of you or the smell of you, and I sure as hell don't like the sound of you. Git!"

Pearcy looked up, startled and unbelieving. "But, Sam, don't you understand? Vince is goin' to be comin' along any minute now with his shotgun, aimin' to kill you dead. I'm doin' you a big favor. You oughtent to be so ungrateful as to chase me off like a yellow dog!"

Sam spat into the dust by Pearcy's foot. "I've got a gun too," he said softly. "And I'm not too much agin shootin' skunks. So git!"

And as the little man crept away into the woods, Sam unhooked the tractor from the rake and headed for the house in a cloud of dust and grasshoppers. Bud Pearcy watched him go and grinned his foxy grin as he slipped into a thicket, where he would have a ringside seat.

"Go right on, Mr. High-and-Mighty," he whispered. "Git your gun. Load it up. One of you bastards is goin' to be drawin' flies before night. Always lookin' down at me, feelin' so kind and holy about givin' me worn-out things for my folks to wear. Hatin' to give me a little work, so's I can buy groceries. Go right ahead and kill each other. I'll be watchin'.''

When Sam returned, he hooked up to the hay rake again and went about his work, but laid across the gearbox of the tractor was a loaded shotgun. Time strung out, long and thin, as the afternoon wore away. The man in the thicket dozed off. The man on the tractor drove with one eye on the windrow and one on the woods path.

And when the shadows had begun to stretch out across the field from the west woods, Vince came walking from the east and stood at the fence.

Sam shut off the ignition and stepped down from the tractor in one motion. With the gun in the crook of his arm, he sauntered toward his neighbor. "'Lo, Vince," he said. "Going hunting?"

The man whitened under his tan. "You know why I've got this gun, Sam," he said. "Bud told me you threatened me, and I'm not one to stay at home and wait for somebody to come after me. If you want to kill me, well here I am. You don't have to go lookin' for me."

Sam drew a long breath. "Bud was here too. Told me that you were gunnin' for me. Can't you see that he's been playin' with both of us? He's too lazy and too mean to amount to a hill of burnt beans, but he's dead jealous of anybody who gets out and digs and accumulates something. Go home and put away the gun, Vince." Sam turned and headed for the tractor.

Some instinct made him stop in his tracks, turning slowly. The shotgun was aimed dead for his middle; Vince's finger was on the trigger. Sam bowed his head and waited, as the finger tightened, bit by bit.

Then it fell away from the trigger, as a look of amazement crossed Vince's face, mixed with sudden agony. He hunched as he went to his knees, his hands pressed to the center of his chest. His head went back, his pale eyes wide in his suddenly colorless face. He stared up at Sam.

Sam dropped his own gun and hurried forward, his hands outstretched. Before he could reach the fence, Vince gave a gasp. His right hand reached toward his old friend, but it found instead the barbed wire. He caught at it, in a last spasm.

The entire strand hummed tautly along the length of the fence. The grip loosed, and the hand fell limp from the wire. The light of the sun, setting red in the west, shone along the length of the fence, dyeing the metal the color of blood.

Jealousy is a dreadful fault, and ignorance is the catalyst that causes nasty effects. If Browning's "My Last Duchess" had lived in East Texas, this might have been what happened to her.

CRAWFISH

It's chill down there in the river, I reckon. She don't know, though. Can't know. Them big, innocent brown eyes are starin' away down there, unless the crawfish...God, I wish I didn't know nothin' about crawfish.

She's got this soft white skin, like to a baby rabbit or some baby animal, sort of. It shined, even through the muddy old river water. I could see her, shinin' and shinin', as she sank. Her hair moved all out loose on the water, dark and curling in the moonlight. It kept moving in the water, all the way down...them crawfish....

She was a tramp, I tell you. Everybody knowed it, I reckon. Smiling and smiling at everybody went by. I moved way down in the bottom-lands, 'count of that. No fancy traveling salesmen comes down here. No Avon women selling damnation. No men in cars and men in trucks that'd look at her when she worked out in the yard. Bending over, showing her legs. Tramp, just tramp!

Must of been born that way. She was just fourteen when I hitched up with her and hadn't had time to learn nothing about men then. Just naturally bad, flirting when we went into town, smilin' at them tellers in the bank, in their white shirts and city suits. Looking with eyes of lust and fornication at them. First time, when I got her home, I beaten the living daylights outen her.

Way she cried and took on, you'd of reckoned she was crazy. Her Pa never had no gumption with his women-folks. Let 'em have their own way clear to ruination, seems like. His woman even had money to spend, when she felt like it. So I guess Mattie wasn't all the way to blame for her sinful ways.

Still, beating didn't do no good—not to last. She'd go round with her head down and her eyes on the ground, like is fitten, for a while. Then she'd see something, maybe just a flower or a bird or some such sinful uselessness. All that decency would be gone in a minute, and she'd be laughin' to herself. And when she laughed, any man inside a mile would be starin' at her like they knowed her already.

I come home one evenin' and she was full of talk. Met me at the door, jabbering fit to make me deaf. I slapped her a couple of times and quieted her down, like as my Pa used to my Ma, iffen she said more than is fitten for a woman. She didn't say nothin' else, just slapped the supper on the table and went off in the back to the garden and started pullin' weeds. I looked round to make sure she wasn't meetin' nobody, afore I set down to eat.

Next day, Miz Rogers, down the road, met me at the end of the row and asked me, real sly like, who'd been visitin' Mattie yesterday. Seemed like I got hot all over—it just seemed to rise up from my feet clean to my head, and I was so mad I could of busted. Miz Rogers—she looked at me kind of scared-like and took off afore I could answer.

It was away before noon, but I took the mules in and unhitched. When I got to the house, she was gigglin' in the kitchen. I crept up, real sly like, and peeped in. They wasn't no one there. She was crazy, clean crazy, and a whore too.

I slammed the screen open till the spring busted. My head was like to bust too, with the blood poundin' and poundin'. She looked round and turned white and funny-lookin'. After she picked herself up from where I knocked her, I started tellin' her what she was. The Whore of Babylon was nice to what I called her.

I slapped all her lies back into her teeth. She was gabblin' about flat tires and women with thirsty children, but she quit that soon enough. She wasn't so all-fired pretty after I got through with her. Her nose was all lopsided and her eyes was so swole you couldn't see what color they was. I figgered, Hell, I might as well of married a homely woman, iffen I was goin' to have to keep mine all bunged up to keep the men away from her.

Next day I went down to see Pa. Didn't let on what was goin' on, but Pa, he's read the Bible and helled around some, so he guessed pretty close. He told me he knowed of some land that was for rent, down close to the river. Said iffen I wanted, he could find somebody to take over my place and finish my crop. It was still early in the spring, so's I had time to make a crop down there in the wet land.

So we moved. There was a fair cabin on the place. Not fancy... she started sayin' something about havin' to carry water so fur, but I just had to look at her mean by then, and she shut right up. I broke a garden patch, and she put in a nice garden, but seemed like she didn't care iffen it growed or not. She didn't put no more flowers round the front neither, so's I knowed she'd done it, t'other place, just to bend over and show her legs to the men on the road. She didn't fix up the cabin none, either. Just went around like she was listenin' to somethin' inside her head. Her Maw come, a time or two, but I didn't care about havin' her come round givin' Mattie fancy notions, so I got rid of her quick as I could.

Got so I hated to come in after finishin' work. I'd stay out till dark, near, or go night-fishin' with the niggers down the river. She kind of looked at me like I was somethin' scary. Give me funny feelin's, the way she looked at me.

No sir, when I took her where she couldn't go smilin' at the men and flirtin' all over town on Saturday no more, she kind of dried up. Never even tried to talk to me no more. I might even of let her, so's to liven up the quiet some, but she kept her lips tight shut over her broke tooth and let the mosquitoes buzz.

Her eyes got queerer an' queerer. They was big to start with, but it got so that they was deep as the pool down at the river and just as full of strange things. I'd go in at night and she'd watch me, starin' and starin' like I was a bug or a snake. She was crazy, I tell you.

Anyways, one evening I come in dead tired. Crop was laid by and I'd been fishin' all day, but it was so hot it like to of took your breath. They wasn't no air down there, 'count of the woods just closed in all round like walls and kept it out.

While I was eatin' supper, she was standin' by the wash-pan, waitin' for the dishes. All of a sudden, she turned round with the meat knife in her hand and started for me. Iffen I hadn't of looked up, she'd of killed me where I set. Seems like, when she done that, everything just come together, like. I took her round the neck and shut my hands tight and when I opened 'em up she was dead. My folks has always been mighty proud and upstandin' people, round here. And Pa—why it'd kill Pa iffen they hung me over a woman. So I took her through the woods down to the river.

I could hear the snakes slidin' off in front of me, while I carried her down the path. The 'gators was bellowin', and the moon was comin' up full. It was right hard gettin' her down the bank to the deep water. She was right smart tall, if she was so slim. I got her down, though, and tied on some weights offen the nets we'd been settin' that day. They wasn't too heavy, but nobody never come there no way. So I put her down in the water. And she sunk slow, and the moon made her go down shinin' and shinin', real soft, like a dream.

Wasn't till the next day I started thinkin' about them crawfish. Iffen you never seen a body that's been et by crawfish, you don't want to. It's a sight to turn a goat's stomach, let alone a man's. I kept thinkin' about her down there, with them things eatin' out her eyes, nibblin' on that soft skin. Seems like I couldn't rightly stand it. For two days I held myself down. I took out and went with the niggers down the river and never come back till the morning of the third day. This morning...seems like forever.

Something drug me down there to the big pool. It's like I couldn't help myself at all. And when I got there, I couldn't see nothin'. I would of thought she'd of riz some by then. Seems like I had to see what they'd done to her, though. Thinkin' was a lot worse than knowin'. I took a sweetgum sapling and started dedgin' around in the deep water, wadin' out as fur as I could. I didn't want to, couldn't hardly stand it, but something made me keep pokin' and feelin' around with that pole, till it caught her.

Must've been caught on a snag or something, cause when the pole hooked her, up she come, slow and easy, just like she gone down. And I throwed up in the water until my insides like to of come out my mouth. Then I had to go and git rocks and rope and sink her good, so's I couldn't never see what they'd done to her, never no more.

I guess I must've went off my head, like. I come to wanderin' round in the woods, all black and blue from bumpin' into things. I went back to the house, but it stared at me outen its windows till I couldn't even go nigh it. Then I went up to Pa's. Course I didn't tell him nothin' about what had happened, but I could see him wonderin'. He loaned me a clean pair of khakis and five dollars, and I come on into town. Seems like I had to see people, be away from the woods.

First thing you know, Will Pollard come up and winked. "Got a jug hid out in the back of the hardware store," he says.

So I went with him. Guess he didn't get much of that jug. I must've drunk most of it. Next thing I remember, Will was lookin' at me with his eyes bugged out and his face fish-belly white.

And now you've got me locked up in here, and they're all down there right now, fixin' to drag her out. And you're lookin' at me like I was the one that was crazy and sinful. And they're goin' to see what I seen when she come up.

Damn them crawfish!

Even criminals aren't safe in the Big Thicket. It's an unforgiving place, complete with many kinds of painful death.

THE WALLOW

It had been raining in the swamp for a week. The hurricane out in the Gulf had come ashore down on the Coast and worn out its worst strength on the low-lying country there. It had sent rain in buckets and bathtubs-full up country, along with a few random tornadoes.

Even in dry weather, the swamp was a hard place to find any dry land. Now there didn't seem to be a spot to put a foot on anyplace.

Golly-Gene dipped his paddle and sent his square-nosed boat between two big hickories. In normal times, they stood on a small knoll of dry land. Now they were standing in water almost up to their lowest branches. Two water moccasins lay along those limbs, dipping their wicked little heads down to see what he was doing.

He frowned up at them and spat a stream of tobacco-juice over the side of the boat. He'd been bit by moccasins time and again, till he was mighty nigh immune to their poison, but he still hated them. The look of them, the stink of them like rotten watermelon. He hated to have to duck his head and go under those branches, feeling the small cold eyes focused on the back of his head. The idea of having a moccasin down his back didn't make him a bit happy.

To avoid them, he would have had to go away out of his way to avoid the tangle of huckleberry bushes and sawvines on either hand. He didn't have the time for that.

While there never was what you'd call a crowd of people messing around in the swamp at any time, and a lot fewer than usual under the present circumstances, he knew that as sure as he needed privacy, he was sure and certain to find people looking over his shoulder. Always had been that way.

That seemed to be a rule of nature. With a dead body in the

back of the boat, it was just best all around to avoid anyplace where people might be. He glanced back to make sure that Cal hadn't moved, that he was truly and surely dead. The boat bumped the tree trunk on his right, and the slack body shifted slightly.

Golly-Gene shivered. It had looked natural, but he knew it wasn't. He'd put a crease behind Cal's left ear that trenched right into his skull. There was no way that bastard could still be alive.

He put his hand over his shirt pocket, felt the button to make sure it was in place. That was purely too much money to let pass you by, given the chance to lay your hands on it.

He pushed the boat away from the hickory with his hand and eased it between the big boles. Beyond the trees and the submerged knoll was the wide pool of clear water that would lead him a long distance without much debris to contend with. Beyond it, where he could see a line of cypresses through the rain, was the maze of runnels and low ridges he wanted to reach. Anything dumped there would never come to light again, for there was a gator wallow somewhere inside that tangle.

Many a night he had run his trotlines and nets and heard the big bulls bellowing their challenges to each other and to the world. Once he put Cal out in there, nobody would ever know what happened to him.

There were no appreciable currents among the many channels criss-crossing the swamp, so nothing ever floated out of it. And those gators were always hungry. He'd seen them snap up moccasins swimming across their pools the way a kid would eat a licorice whip. They'd think Cal was a treat, sent especially for them by the storm.

He looked up at the gray pall of cloud hanging low over the swamp. There wasn't any lighter place to tell him where the sun was, but he felt sure it was past mid-afternoon. Still raining, though the downpour had slacked to a slow, sad drizzle.

He laid his paddle aside and picked up the Maxwell House Coffee can. He bailed out a couple of dozen canfuls before he decided it was safe to go on. A waterlogged boat in a flooded swamp wasn't anything to trifle with. He had no intention of adding his own body for dessert, after the gators finished with Cal.

He dumped the last can overboard and wiped his face on his dirty bandana. His hands were white as grub worms from being wet so long. His face felt clammy with sweat and damp. There was no denying that it was getting darker, even out in the open. He knew it would be dismal under the trees beyond the pool.

Dammit, he ought to've waited for morning. But how can you

ever be sure some good old drinking buddy isn't going to come staggering up to the shack and blunder into the shed where he hid Cal's body at first? His drinking buddies were famous for staggering into places where they shouldn't go and doing things they sure as hell shouldn't have done.

He supposed some might have said the same about him, but until today he'd never done anything worse than raping a nigger wench or pilfering goods from the grocery store and the hardware department of the discount stores. He'd lived a pretty fair life, though he knew there were some as would say Golly-Gene Tucker was a low-life and a thief.

He grinned. After today, he was going to make tracks out of the swampy country for good. Go to Houston or Baton Rouge. Set up in business maybe, though he hadn't any notion what business he might try. Five thousand dollars was more money than most of the folks he knew would see in a year's hard work.

The boat bumped hard into a floating log. Cal's body finished shifting and now lay along the bottom of the boat in an impossible position. Golly-Gene looked back again.

"Too bad, old Cal. But you'd have drunk it all up, you know that well as I do. Your old man would still be gone, and so would all that insurance money. Too bad your damn sisters took so much of it—I could go into business in a big way with the whole wad. But I can't fault you for that. You couldn't help having a slew of sisters, no more than I could help having a slut for a ma and a miserable bum for a pa.

"I'd say you done me a mighty good turn. Too bad I can't give you a real bang-up burying, but if you could still think, you'd know I can't risk that."

He drove hard with the paddle, pushing the awkward boat across the slough as fast as he could. The dark line of trees came near, and he picked a clearish channel and went into the dark mass of half-drowned timber. The cypress knees stuck up like teeth, almost invisible against the black water. He had to watch carefully, for they could rip through even a metal boat, if you came at them too fast and from the wrong angle.

It was raining harder again. He peered down at the water in front of the boat and found himself looking into a pair of knobby eyes. Nothing else was visible, but he knew the alligator was there, lying beneath the water, watching what was going on in his territory. He spat another brown stream at the eyes, and they sank instantly from view.

It was misty under the cypresses, a low fog rising from the surface of the water and mingling with the misting rain until you could hardly tell where one left off and the other began. Golly-Gene stood up in the boat, being very careful, and looked ahead.

There it was. The huge water-oak stood on the slight ridge above the wallow, its foliage standing out from that of the cypresses, even in the dimness. Not long now, Cal, he thought, as he sat and began paddling again.

The ridge was out of sight beneath the flood water, but the tree gave him a good bearing. As he came under it, two more moccasins slid along low branches and let their necks droop long to see what he was doing. He hated that cottony maw, like some sort of wicked flower blooming where it had no business being.

The bottom of the boat gave a tearing groan, and water flowed up to his boot-tops before he realized what had happened. He'd ripped the damn boat!

Golly-Gene kicked off those boots before they could take him down. The boat went out from under him, and Cal's body bobbed gently on the surface of the foggy water. He trod water, staring around for someplace to go. Someplace above the water that was, he knew, the wallow of a whole family of gators. There wasn't a dry spot within miles.

Something hit Cal's body, pulling it under in a mighty swashing of waves and blood. Golly-Gene struck out for the oak as fast as he could swim. Every stroke he made he felt that one of the big beasts was coming up behind, ready to take that first and fatal bite.

His skin was crawling. His teeth chattered, and his hands shook as he caught the trunk of the oak and began climbing it, digging toes and fingers into the wet, rough bark.

He touched something that slithered from beneath his hand. He gasped a curse. Damn tree was full of snakes!

He reached the first branching and went out on a limb. It sagged beneath his weight, and he looked down into a pair of bubble-eyes that stared up at him through the mist.

"My God!" said Golly-Gene Tucker.

Not even an echo came back through the flooded swamp.

...And you'd better be careful what you steal, too!

STIFF SENTENCE

It was a bad job, right from the first. Kenny had cased that little bank way out in the boonies—he had a relative that lived in the little bitty town not too far from there, and he never could keep his mind off business, even when visiting his kin. Always had an eye out for the main chance, did Kenny.

Sibley was a place you'd miss if you winked going through it. If you sneezed too, you'd miss everything from the cemetery at one end of town to the school on the other. But Kenny never missed anything. He stopped at the café and listened to the old codgers gossiping.

He learned a lot, like the fact that the bank was one that people for miles around seemed to use, because it was still a country bank that hadn't computerized itself right out of the human race. Your character, for instance, made the difference in making a loan.

The place even sounded good to me, and I intended to help rob it. Of course, Kenny wasn't sentimental about things like that. He got Robert to come in for the inside work, and he located me to tend to the transportation. I've always been good at that: I can hotwire a car faster than most people can crank it with a key.

I usually can figure out and fix what's wrong when one stops running too. Nine times out of ten that's true; it would turn out that the Sibley job would be the tenth time.

Sibley was a bedroom community for a middle-sized industrial town about fifteen or twenty miles up the road. It also had a batch of senior citizens who lived on Social Security and pensions of one kind or another. Around the first of the month, they kept a lot of cash on hand, for the old nesters out in the East Texas woods don't like to pay by check, mostly. They want cash in their hot little hands.... I expect that if they could get ahold of gold, they'd hold out for that.

It made it perfect for our needs. Big banks in cities keep lots of cash on hand, but they also have a lot of trigger-happy security. Little banks may not have more than a hundred thou' in cash, but their security is enough to make a cat laugh.

We planned the hit for the second day of the month, a Monday. All the commuters would be off at work. The oldsters would be heading toward the bank with their checks ready to cash. If we hit early, not long after opening, we felt that we would get the whole pot.

We made the run in a black Chevy I lifted from a used car lot in Houston. It was the sort of car that can run straight over you, and you couldn't describe it if you lived. We had a Buick hid out on a woods road about five miles out on a county oil-top, and it could put us over the Louisiana line in about an hour flat, if things went right.

Naturally, things didn't.

Kenny and Robert came boiling out of the bank's side door with a couple of bags full of cash. I had the engine running, of course, and Kenny yelled, "Hit it, Ray!" before he got the door shut. We took off like scalded cats.

I hooked a left, and we were behind the big trees, out of sight. Then I slowed and doubled back through a field, along a wagon road, and that got us almost to our second car, which was waiting in the woods. We ran the Chevy away back into the thickest part of the timber and shoved it down into a ravine. We pulled brush over all the tracks. Nobody was ever going to find that sucker.

The ski masks and the jackets the two inside men wore went down with it, and we pulled on the coats to our business suits, put the money into leather briefcases, lit up big expensive cigars, and pulled out onto the oil-top. We caught a through highway in five minutes, and from there it should have been smooth sailing.

About a mile outside of Croft (population 7,200), the engine began to overheat. Badly.

I nursed her along, scared to stop, because I felt in my bones that when that engine died even Jesus Christ wasn't going to bring her back to life again. We got to Croft and pulled into the parking lot around a smallish shopping mall. It was just filling up with cars, and that made it a good place to dump a car without its being noticed, maybe for days.

"Ray, you go and lift us some wheels," Kenny said. "We'll go into the mall and mingle. Won't do to stand out here in the open and get noticed."

I could see a couple of service stations from where the car sat. The parking lot was too busy to risk hotwiring anything there, but I thought there might be something that had been washed and serviced and parked out behind one of those stations. Anything to get us out of town would suit me fine.

I locked the briefcases in the Buick. Then I took off my jacket and stuffed my tie in my pocket. Little places like Croft, in hot weather, are not where you find men in suits unless they are from out of town.

The first station was busy, but nothing promising showed up on its parking ramp. Ambling down the street, I kept an eye on the next, which was a big Exxon on a corner. As I watched, a hearse slid up to the pumps and the driver got out and went into the office. I could read his motions—he wanted the thing filled up, oil checked, and parked while he went down the street to the little café for his breakfast.

The boy came out and filled the tank, checked everything, and drove it around to the back of the station, so nobody would run into it. I had it out of the parking ramp before the boy had got himself set down in the office again.

I parked it behind an empty house in an overgrown driveway and walked to the mall after Kenny and Robert and the money. Five minutes later, we were on our way again. Time had been lost, but we still felt we were in good shape.

This time, of course, we became bereaved relatives, instead of hotshot businessmen. We were on our way to the mortuary to pick up Uncle Albert's corpse. We'd gone twenty miles before Kenny said, "Say, did you look into the back of this thing?"

What with one thing and another, I hadn't. We stopped in a dirt track and opened the doors.

We had lifted a stiff! He must've been picked up at a hospital and was on his way to be embalmed—he was still in that skimpy hospital gown. Looked awful too. What was worse, I recognized him—that was the body of Judge Walker Johns, who'd sent me up four times for felony over the past ten years. I thought Kenny would bust a gut—he'd sent him up a few times too.

Robert was almost crying. "This guy's from a big rich family over to Rogersville!" he moaned. "They've got money and own politicians and run things like lords. They'll have everybody in the state looking for him. The feds too—what's the penalty for kidnapping a judge?"

"My God, Robert," I said, "you can't kidnap a stiff. And I dunno as I ever heard of any law against stealing one. You, Ken?"

He shrugged. "No, but that doesn't mean there isn't one. We've got to dump this bird. Someplace where nobody will ever find him or this meat wagon. Then we've got to lift another set of wheels. You idiot, Ray: I'd of thought you would look in the back!"

That made me a little hot. "It was sitting there full of gas, with the driver gone for a good half hour, if not more. You'd have done the same," I protested. But he looked skeptical.

It was a very hot day. Of course, we all knew the man in the back hadn't been dead for more than a few hours. Probably died in the night. But we all kept wrinkling up our noses and I could swear I could begin to smell him. It almost drove us out of our gourds.

We crept through little towns at the speed limit or below, keeping our eyes peeled for a promising set of wheels. Nothing showed; junkers seemed to be all that anybody out in the woods country could afford.

When we got to Dobson, I said, "Let me out here. Go on across the state line and hide the wagon in that big stand of pines four miles past the marker. Wait for me there, back in the woods, while I find something and catch up to you."

I should have known better. When a job goes sour, it goes all the way. They caught me red-handed hotwiring another Buick. Big silver job that looked fast too.

Oh, you can go ahead and look for Kenny and Robert, if you want, but it's already been a long time since they left me. They're not dopes. They've found some way to go on, and if you find 'em in that stand of pines, holding hands with that stiff, they're stupider than I took them for.

I still want to know how you got my description, though. I didn't even go into that tacky little bank, and not a soul even so much as glanced at the Chevy while I waited.

Damn! You don't mean it! An old lady with a telescope? You've got to be kidding. Well, I can sort of see that a little bitty place like that doesn't have much excitement....

How many? Six divorces? My God, I didn't know little towns had so much action going on. She ratted on 'em all, did she? And on me too.

Oh, well. I guess the public defender will do me as well as anybody. My own lawyer gave up on me after the last conviction. He didn't do me any good anyhow.

Too bad—this looked like such an easy job. And with my luck, Kenny and Robert will make it away clean as a whistle, while I'm stuck with the rap again.

It's almost enough to make a man go straight.

Psychosis takes oddball forms in the big woods—and this story is based on a series of actual newspaper stories that aren't that far in the past.

DIGGING UP ARTHUR

Even after ten years, I still kill him again every night. There's no satisfaction in it, of course, because I know I'm dreaming. You'd think, having gotten away with it as slick as a whistle, that I'd let the thing drop, let him be, let him lie there in the cemetery in the woods and rest in peace.

I can't seem to do that. He died too fast. It wasn't slow and painful enough to fulfill the need that made me kill him to begin with. I wish I hadn't taken the gun with me at all. My bare hands would have had the pleasure of wringing his miserable life out of him, cutting off his breath, feeling him struggle and heave, watching him go black in the face.... I get excited when I think about that. Have to go out and walk around the block very quickly, while I cool down again.

I never had the urge to kill anyone else. Not ever. But after he married Linda—my Linda—I never wanted anything so much in my life as to kill Arthur, slowly, painfully, lingeringly...there! My blood pressure is going up again. Have to watch that.

I go about my business just about the way anyone else does; take my wife and children to church and to picnics and ballgames. I'm no monster. I don't let that fixation get in the way of earning a living and helping out my neighbors. I even ran for the City Council last year, though I was pretty relieved when I was beaten in the run-off.

It's just about this time of year, late summer, with the grass drying in the fields and pears getting ripe on the trees, the heat wavering in a haze over everything, that I think of that last day of Arthur's life. It all came to a head that day, though he didn't have the foggiest notion that I had ever been upset with him at all, anymore than anyone else had.

I walked up to him in the back woods behind his farmhouse. He thought I'd been out hunting rabbits, I suppose, because he didn't more than glance at the shotgun I carried.

I blew him away before he could finish saying hello.

Everyone, including the deputies and the sheriff, thought somebody had been hunting in the woods, and had killed him by accident and been afraid to own up to it. There was a big funeral, and I took Carrie and the baby and we all looked mighty sad.

I thought I had done with him.

The dreams started a while later. I'd wake up out of a sound sleep, covered with sweat, seeing him dying. Not by the shotgun blast, but in a lot of different ways, all of them slow. Carrie began to believe I was coming down with something and kept giving me vitamins. There would be months and months when everything went along fine as silk. Then I'd get to thinking about Arthur. I'd go out there to Rosebud Cemetery, whenever Carrie took the kids to see her mother for a few days, and do nothing but drink, lying there on Arthur's grave, cursing him better and better the drunker I got.

The cemetery is so far out in the woods that nobody goes there except for a funeral or, from time to time, to put a plot in order. There's plenty of warning—you can hear a car rattling over the washboard road for a mile or more before it gets there, so I never got caught. But after a while it got so that that wasn't enough.

I went all over the area, when I could steal the time from my job, and tore down his advertising stickers for his real estate business that he ran along with his farm. Got every one in the county and most of those in the adjoining counties. That helped for a good long time, because it wasn't a thing you can get done in a year or even in two.

I quit having the dreams as long as that lasted, but there came a time when I couldn't find a sign or a sticker or even a business card left anyplace. That's when the dreams started again.

I knew something had to be done when I woke up in the middle of the night choking Carrie. She was grunting and struggling and flopping, and that must be what woke me. Good thing. I'd have killed her if I'd gone on sleeping.

That really put the fat into the fire. Nothing would do but I had to go to Dallas and see a psychiatrist. She harped on that day and night until I wished I'd finished the job—or at least broken her voice box. I had good reason not to take off from work, but finally she got at Ralph, my boss, and the two of the fixed it up so I had to go.

That was one screwed-up dude I talked to. When I told him I

was having bad dreams, he got started on why I hated my folks and when I'd been toilet trained. Soon as I saw what he wanted, I gave him just that, and he sent me home with a clean bill of health. Well, not quite that, but he said I was as normal as anybody. Which, looking around me, doesn't say a lot at that.

This thing had been rocking along for a decade by now, and I'd handled it as well as I could all the way. The cemetery quit being used for new burials, so I could visit there without having to fear anything but a visit from Arthur's old mother, who had a habit of going out there and weeding or planting flowers at the damndest times.

I don't know if it was choking Carrie or the talk with the psychiatrist that got things off their even keel. I started having worse dreams than ever. I made so much noise at night that Carrie moved into the guest room, just to be able to sleep.

I'd wake up in a cold sweat, with my hands remembering the throbbing of Arthur's throat or feeling the sticky heat of his blood, and I'd lie there shaking for a long time. I soon knew that something had to be done. I hadn't done it right in the beginning, that was the problem. What I had to do now was to do it all over again, and this time do a bang-up job. It would take time. Uninterrupted time. In the daylight. I wasn't about to try something like that in the dark.

My chance came when Carrie's Ma got sick. It was late summer again, with the kids out of school, so they all went to stay for a couple of weeks and get the old lady back on her feet. If she'd known what a favor she was doing me, she'd have got well right off, instead of going around so puny for so long. But she didn't know, and that's what counts.

I watched Arthur's Ma for a few days, to make sure she'd already done her stint of graveyard tending for the week. Sure enough, she got done on a Tuesday. I went home from work Wednesday with a virus, I told Ralph. Wouldn't be in the next day at all. Maybe by Friday....

He was all sympathy.

* * * * * * *

Bright and early Thursday morning I took off for Rosebud Cemetery in the old pickup that belonged to my Dad. I keep it out in the back shed, and it only gets cranked once a month. It had enough tools in the back to dig up the whole graveyard.

They'd put in a fancy kind of grave marker. Out at Rosebud, the graves are all so old, most of them, that they just go anywhichaways.

The plots lie at angles to each other, and there's no telling, except by the individual markers, which way any grave is headed. I checked out Arthur's pretty carefully, but I have to admit that I'd brought a bottle to keep me company.

I decided which end was which, and that wasn't easy, and started in digging. I didn't intend to uncover the whole coffin, you see, but just a hole big enough to let me get down and choke him again through the hole I'd chop in the lid. Saved a heck of a lot of work.

Well, I worked and sweated, and the sun got hotter and hotter above the big pines that shaded the place, and I kept drinking to help cool off. But it was near noon by the time I hit something that went thunk! It was the coffin, and no mistake.

I climbed out of the hole and got my hatchet, which I'd brought just for that purpose. Once back down there, I began hacking away at the coffin-lid. They don't make those things with chopping in mind. They're slick and hard, and that had been an expensive box.

Finally I broke through, and that gave me the energy to get busy and make that hole big enough so I could see his ugly face while I did the job right and choked him.

By damn, when I looked through with my flashlight, there was nothing there but a pair of skinny ankles in black silk socks! I'd gone and dug up the wrong end!

I tried choking the ankles, but it just isn't the same thing. Besides, there was a smell. I could have stood it, if I'd been really caught up in what I was doing, but it just wasn't going to work. I could see that pretty soon.

There was no way I could take the time to dig up the other end and chop through more of that confounded coffin. I didn't have the time, I didn't have the energy, and I was hot as a six-shooter anyway. Having a stroke or heart attack out there at Rosebud wasn't going to help things a bit.

That's why I came back home without doing what I'd set out to do. That's not my way, not as a general rule, but things just turned out so.

I'm lying here in my E-Z-Rest with a cold beer in my hand and the TV on. I'll get all good and rested. Tomorrow morning, I'll call in and tell Ralph I'm still sick.

Then, by God, I'll go back out there and dig up the right end of Arthur!

There are wild tales about cougars still floating about in the woods of East Texas. But the very wildest ones are probably true....

NIGHT OF THE COUGAR

She watched Jody as long as she could see the glint of his red shirt through the leaves along the brushy trail. The dim thuds of old Sam's shoes came to her ears for a little while longer. Then they were both gone, and the birdcalls in the woods around the cabin didn't seem to interrupt the silence at all.

Julie sighed as she turned toward her garden plot. With Little Jody and the baby both napping, her house was quiet too. She had always liked the woodsy spot they'd picked to homestead. East Texas was much like her southern Mississippi birthplace, but when Jody went off in work with the loggers it got mighty lonesome.

Her sunbonnet was hot against her neck, and its curving brim cut off her view of anything around her when she stooped over the rows, her hands busy among the tender sprouts of cabbage and turnip greens and onions. She didn't really like sunbonnets...never had. It had taken the full weight of her father's authority to make her toe the line and wear one to keep the sun from browning her fair skin.

"'Tain't ladylike!" had been his most devastating indictment of any female. But she had never liked the girls he pointed out as ideals of feminine behavior. It was just as well that Jody had come along and carried her away from Laurel and its cadre of ladylike prototypes.

There was motion—she turned her head to watch a coachwhip snake go slipping along the fence line by the woodshed. No danger there, she knew.

But she kept a wary eye on any serpent about the house. Little Jody was at an age when anything new got chased and usually caught. She had no intention of letting him get bit by a copperhead or a moccasin.

The late spring sun was warm on her back. Sweat began sliding down her beneath her wool serge clothing. It was time to get out the summer-weight stuff, to cut Jody out of his winter underwear. She'd shed her own three weeks ago, amid her husband's dire warnings about late cold snaps and pneumonia.

Then the sweat all but all but congealed on her skin. A long wail cut across the morning woods-noises. A cougar, hunting late maybe. She hated the sound of them, the long lonesome cry like a woman in pain. And once she'd been warned about the beast, she had hated it even more. A creature that craved human babies was something downright evil.

There were tales among the old women she saw occasionally at camp meetings of the church in the summertime; they could tell you tales that would curl your hair and kink your bones. One of those women had lost her own babe some forty years gone, when a cougar had come right into the yard and taken it out of the basket where it was sleeping while she washed. Julie shivered, remembering.

Though she knew better, she put away her hoe and went into the house to check on the children. Little Jody slept in total relaxation, boneless, his small month open, his eyes partway open too. Lissa was beginning to squirm in her hickory-splint basket, the way she always did when she was getting ready to wake up. It was just as well she'd quit in the garden. The baby would be ready to nurse any minute now. And Jody would wake up hungry. He always did.

The infant whimpered. Julie bent over the crib, felt the dampish head. Lissa hadn't been feeling too pert for some time now. Likely some spring ailment. She'd make up some herb tea and spoon it down the child. Everybody needed a tonic in the spring, seemed like.

She lifted the plump baby and sat in the small rocker she'd brought from Mississippi in the wagon with the rest of their few bits of furniture and Jody's plow-tools. Unbuttoning her bodice let in a grateful bit of cool air as the baby suckled. Before they were done, Jody began to grunt and thrash, the way he did sometimes. Seemed as if a body needed to be twins, when you had so much to do.

She didn't put the children in the little pen their daddy had built in the front yard, when both were fed. She'd heard that cougar, and she was no fool. She kept them in sight all afternoon, though it meant taking off her ladylike sunbonnet and putting on her husband's old straw hat while she finished up in the garden.

Jody was fine, just playing with pine cones and marking in the dust with sticks and watching Coaly, the fiery black horse, pace 'round and 'round the lot where he was penned. But Lissa wasn't herself. She whimpered a lot, gave little bubbling cries from time to time. Julie began to feel uneasy about her. Something was amiss, and Jody had always been so healthy that she hadn't learned much about baby sickness in dealing with him.

There was a quiver of uneasiness inside her at the thought. With her husband gone and the nearest neighbor twelve miles east, through woods so thick you couldn't see ten feet in any direction, it was scary to contemplate what she'd do if one of the children got really badly sick. She had tackled a lot of hard things since leaving home and her mother. She shook herself, took a deep breath.

Nobody had ever promised her it'd be easy, Jody least of all. In fact, he'd stressed everything he could think of that might have made her change her mind. He'd wanted her to marry him, no doubt of that, but he'd had no intention of taking her off to something that wasn't what she thought it'd be. She couldn't fault him for the fact that there'd been things that neither of them had been able to guess at.

Like the lack of doctors. There wasn't one nearer than Nicholson, twenty-five miles to the west. It was pure luck that had put them as near as they were to Gramma Dooley, though twelve miles was a long way and took a half day to cover, with the road nothing more than a rough track through the woods. On horseback it was quicker, but if she were forced to make it there on her own she'd have to take the buckboard. You just couldn't manage a baby and a three-year-old on horseback. Particularly when the horse was Coaly.

She finished in the garden and took the children inside. It was mid-afternoon, already hot and steamy, though it was only April. She took the cotton clothing out of the long chest and shook it out, then hung it on the clothesline to air. The heavier woolens they'd worn all winter had already been washed or aired and gone into storage. By the time she finished it was twilight.

When she was fixing Jody's supper, nibbling along as she did it, as she usually did for her own meals, she heard a sound from the sleeping room where she'd put Lissa back into her basket. A choking sound.

Her heart thumping in her throat, Julie ran across the dog-run hall and caught up the baby. The child's fare was scarlet, and she was struggling for breath. As she lifted her, Lissa began coughing harshly, wheezing for breath between spasms. A dose of honey and vinegar didn't relieve the baby's coughing. The struggles to breathe made the baby try to cry, and that made everything even worse. The herb tea didn't seem to help at all, nor did goose grease rubbed onto her chest. By full dark, Julie knew that she needed help.

She hitched Coaly by lantern light. Crickets were chittering all around in the grass. Frogs of all sizes were chorusing down at the creek. A screech owl's shivering cry punctuated the rest, making her shiver. But she didn't hear the cougar. That was something she was thankful for.

She put blankets in the wagon bed for Little Jody. He was almost asleep when she laid him on them, and by the time she came back with Lissa in her basket he was sound asleep. The baby was still making those strange barking sounds. She seemed to have a fever too, though Julie was so hot with haste and work that it was hard to tell.

She hung the lantern on the hook let into the pole at the front of the wagon, led Coaly out into the track that went roughly upward past their front porch, and climbed into the buckboard.

"Hup! Coaly, giddap!" she said, and the horse snorted, tried to dance sideways between the shafts, then reluctantly moved forward. The night air was so much cooler than the afternoon had been that it felt almost cold to her hands. She tugged the spare quilt she'd brought for Jody about her shoulders and smacked the hors's rump with the end of a rein.

The forest was in darkness, deeper than the moonless sky. Leaves shone fitfully as the lantern passed, but the feeble gleam couldn't penetrate far into the dense wood on either side of the track. And the track itself took much of her attention. Coaly's neat hooves could pass easily over ruts and roots that jounced the wagon so hard it endangered its wheels.

Her eyes soon ached with the effort to see ahead, to guide the horse around the worst of the bad spots in the road. She was tired to the bone too, for her day had been work from beginning to end. But she wasn't sleepy, no matter how her eyes protested or her body ached. She heard every effortful breath her baby drew, flinched at every wheeze or coughing spasm.

The night seemed to pass as slowly as the miles. She had no clock, but the stars moved in a narrow ribbon above the cut where the track ran, and she could tell, when she looked, that the constellations were progressing westward. But so slowly!

She figured that she was somewhere about halfway to her destination when she heard the cry again. Like a woman screaming. The cougar! Had the beast been following her all that distance? Silently creeping behind the slow-paced wagon, drawn by the scent of her child?

Coaly was tired raw, though she had stopped twice to let him drink at creeks they'd crossed and once to let him rest a bit. But she sat straighter and flicked him with the reins. He snorted with irritation, but he picked up his hooves a bit faster.

Julie felt beneath the rough plank-board seat and found the handle of the bullwhip Jody kept for running the stock out of her garden. Coaly had never in his life felt the weight of that four-ply lash, but she knew that the time might well be coming when he would.

Behind them there was another sound—not the scream now, but a rough, coughing growl. As if in answer, the baby went into a fit of coughing that seemed as if it would tear out her tender lungs. She found no relief until Julie reached down, one-handed, and lifted Lissa into her lap. Lying on her stomach, head down, the child gave a last choking wheeze and got a lungful of air.

Having to secure Lissa on her knees added one more burden to Julie's load. Coaly was moving faster, bouncing the wagon over obstacles she hadn't the time to pick out and steer around. Behind her in the wagon bed Jody was whimpering, still half asleep but disturbed by the rough jolting of the wagon.

"Go back to sleep, baby," she said over her shoulder. "We'll be there soon."

The little boy reached up to catch a handful of her skirt that hung over the back of the seat-board. "I don't like it, Mama," he said. "Don't like to sleep in the wagon. Don't like goin' in the dark. Less go home. Please?"

"We'll be at Gramma Dooley's in a little while. You like Gramma—remember when we went to the revival and she gave you the horehound candy? She'll likely have some more for you. And sugar cookies. You know how you like her cookies!"

The wagon lurched over part of a stump left in the track, and Jody forgot about cookies and began to howl in earnest. As Julie spared a glance back, she thought she saw something in the track. It was too dark to tell what, and it was a long way back, but there was a deeper darkness there. Moving.

"Jody!" she grated, her voice harsher than he had ever heard it. "Shut your mouth! Lie down and roll up in the blanket! And be still. I'm not playing any game. There's a cougar back there, I'm pretty sure. We've got to move fast, and it's going to be mighty rough. Now you do like I tell you!"

When he had rolled into a dark lump, she reached down and lifted the lantern from its hook. Then, holding the baby against her with both knees, keeping the reins in her left hand, she turned, holding the light high, and looked fully backward.

Two reddish sparks glinted with reflected light. Then they blinked once and were gone. So was the shadow, but she knew the animal had taken to the trees. It could travel as quickly through that tangle as Coaly could along the roadway. There was no way a horse could outrun a cougar while pulling a buckboard, even if it had a good surface to run on. But she had to try to make Coaly do the impossible.

She put the lantern back in its place. One-handed, jouncing and bumping as she worked, she put the baby into the basket on the seat beside her and tied that securely to the braces holding the seat in place. Then she swung the bullwhip in a long arc overhead and cracked its wicked tip just above the black horse's nervous ears.

"Go, Coaly! Whup!"

Coaly went. Faster than she'd have thought he could, burdened as he was. The wagon seemed to leap into the air as it cleared a big bump, and it hit with a tooth-rattling jar. Jody cried out, and she heard him scrambling for a handhold.

Around blind curves, through masses of foliage that had leaned forward into the track the horse flew, and the wagon bounced along behind as best it could. Julie had her feet hooked into the seat-brace beneath her, reins clenched uselessly in her left hand, while her right steadied the basket and the baby.

When the scream sounded again it was entirely too close. Behind the wagon...but not by much. She risked a glimpse back, and a shadow was flowing along with the wild shapes cast by the swinging lantern. When the wagon-shadow bounced and jumped, the other moved smoothly and steadily, not ten feet from the tailboard!

Julie was thinking faster than ever before. The creature wanted Lissa. That was what all the folktales suggested...unless it wanted Coaly. They liked horsemeat too. But she felt sure it would prefer something tender...and human. What if she could distract it? Throw something out that it could smell baby-scent on?

She took the reins in her teeth and dug into the basket, pulled out a soiled diaper, and flung it over the side of the careening buckboard. Then she cracked the whip again.

But by now Coaly had caught scent of the big cat, and the horse's instinct told him what words could not. The stocky black had leaned his chest into his work and was making his former pace look slow. It was all Julie could do to keep from being flung out into the darkness, and nothing but the basket straps kept Lissa from being dislodged from her place. Jody was rolling around in the wagon bed, too frightened to whimper.

They flew along the track for a half mile before Julie pulled Coaly down a bit...enough so she could risk another look to their rear. The other shadow was gone. For now. She had no illusion that the cat would waste much time on the diaper, once it was sure it was empty.

With the horse under some control, she tore through the woods. And now she was able to see some landmarks that told her she was getting nearer her goal. The immense oak tree that leaned over the track—that was less than three miles from the Dooleys' house. With any luck at all, they just might make it. She cracked the whip again, but not quite so close to Coaly's sensitive ears. He kept moving, but he wasn't bolting now.

"Jody...how are you making it, son?" she asked.

"M...M...Mama...there was a great big *something* back there!"

She made her voice matter-of-fact. "Yes. That was the cougar. Remember...I told you, just before we went so fast."

"Oh. I didn't know they were so *big*. It was like Aunt Till's tomcat, but lots and lots bigger. It was scary, Mama."

"Well, it didn't get us...yet. And it won't, I think. I believe I've figured out the combination. You just get a good grip on the seat-braces and you watch for it for me. Its eyes will shine in the light that gets back there from the lantern. You sing out if you see it coming after us again."

"Yes'm." His voice sounded as frightened as Julie felt.

The wagon went swaying and jangling and creaking around more bends in the track, and Julie had begun to hope they'd left the beast far behind when Jody's warning came.

"It's there, Mama!" he shouted.

Once more the thing neared the tailboard, its shadow mingling with those of the wagon and its passengers. Again she picked a bit of cloth from the basket and pitched it into the road. And they gained another half-mile or so.

There was the skillet nailed to the ash tree, set there as a marker of the trail by some long-dead explorer of the region. It gleamed rust-red in the lantern light for an instant. Only a mile left to go. And then the wagon hit something with an ominous *c-r-a-a-ck*! The right front wheel went, and the bed pitched forward at an angle.

Even as Julie went over the side, she was trying to see behind, to see if the cougar was there again. She was up almost before she hit the ground, rescuing the lantern from its hook, unhooking Coaly from the harness.

"Jody! Climb down, son. That's right...come here to me. You're going to ride Coaly, you know that? Do you think you can ride him?"

"But Daddy said he's too uppity for me!"

"Ordinarily, that's true. But this is something out of the ordinary. You're not only going to ride him, you're going to see to

Lissa, too. See? I'm tying her basket right here onto his back with the harness straps. You can hook your legs right into here...that's right. Whoa, Coaly. Easy, boy." She settled the two children into her makeshift rig of hamstrings and bits of harness, checked it out for security, then stepped back.

"You head right up the track, Jody. You can see where it is by the stars, and Coaly isn't going out into the brush, and he certainly isn't coming back here where the cat is. I'll be right behind you with the lantern. But you make him *run*, you hear me? Kick him with your heels. Slap him with the reins. Go, now!" and she struck the horse sharply with the stock of the whip she had taken from the wreck of the wagon.

As the hoofbeats rattled away up the red-dirt track, she turned where she stood and held the lantern high. No eyes sparked at her... yet. She backed slowly up the way, watching sharply. Then she turned and ran as hard as she could for a couple of hundred yards. When she turned again there were red points of light there in the road.

Julie's heart thumped high in her throat. Beads of sweat sprang out along her hairline, as she watched the tawny shape that she saw clearly now for the first time.

The cat was cautious. An adult human being wasn't its usual prey, and the fire in the lantern filled its eyes disturbingly. But its gut growled with hunger. Julie could see the creature weighting its hunger against the unknown threat she might pose.

Before it could make up its mind, she was upon it, the whip swinging down in a wicked arc, the metal tip cracking viciously as it drew blood that showed bright against the tan coat. The cougar crouched, snarling, its ears flat against its head, its eyes glaring. But Julie was past caution. To buy time for her children she was prepared to risk everything. She danced to one side and cracked the whip again. Another trickle of blood gleamed against the creature's neck.

The lantern that she had hung on a stub of branch beside the track gave her enough light for maneuvering, and she struck again as the beast backed away, keeping its head toward her, its eyes focused on her as the pressing danger it knew it faced.

Then a rain of whip strokes drove the creature backward into the edge of the wood...deeper. And then it was gone, a frustrated cough of anger coming back to Julie's ears as the last twitch of brush marked its passage.

Julie listened hard. The only sounds were tree frogs, a whip-poor-will in the distance, a hoot owl somewhere nearby, and the many small noises of a wood at night. There was no scream to be heard, nor any other sound that might mark the hunt of a big cat.

She turned in her track, the lash of the whip marking the red dust of the road. She took the lantern from the stub.

Now she could hear sounds from the road ahead. Men's voices, calling...but she was suddenly too exhausted to make a sound. The children were safe...that was all that mattered. If they hadn't reached Dooleys', nobody would be calling in the forest in the early morning hours.

Letting the lantern dangle wearily from her hand, dragging the whip, she started up the trail toward the east. The early morning constellations hung above the cut. A mockingbird was tuning up his song in the woods.

Our little bank in the town near which we live was robbed several years ago by real pros. I wish there had been a Lena McCarver in the woods to give them their comeuppance....

THE PUSHOVER

It looked like a piece of cake. Mel and I had knocked over six little country banks without a hitch, though if course the FBI had makes on us, and our pictures were out all over the map. Hell, this little old bank had them posted—I saw them when I cased it a couple of days before the job. Nobody gave me more of a second glance than a stranger in a back-country town gets anyway.

We had it down pat, with a car stashed in the woods a couple of miles from a three-way crossroad, the timing worked out to a second, everything smooth as oil. When we busted into the side door of the bank and all the people froze with surprise and fear, we worked it right to schedule. In three minutes we were in number one car and moving, with well over fifty thousand dollars in the bags at our feet.

That was when things came unglued. Somebody must have slid out the front door when we came in the side, for an old codger behind a beat-up pickup let loose on us with a double-barreled shotgun. It didn't stop the car or hurt either of us, but it made hash of the windshield, and that slowed us down getting to the second car.

The police band scanner in the car saved our bacon. We had thought we'd have plenty of time to get clear before the nearest law could get thirty miles out into the country and get descriptions of us. Just bad luck made a deputy be cruising the highway three miles away. He'd have had us, without that scanner. As it was, we had to ditch number two car and take to the woods in a hurry.

Those are big damn woods down there. Undergrowth is so thick you can hardly plow through, some places. But there's lots of creeks and quite a bit of swampy land, so we felt as if we could throw off the bloodhounds that were sure to be put on our trail. Both of us are country boys and know the woods like the palms of our hands. Besides, we stopped in the middle of an overgrown field and scrubbed ourselves down, shoe-soles and all, with goatweeds. That ought to change the scent of anything that walks.

We'd had all sorts of supplies packed in number two, so we had with us enough food for a good while, with blankets, all rolled into easily carried bundles. But what with sawvines and huckleberry thickets, we were glad to find a spot that we figured would do us until the heat died down. It was a low ridge rising out of a sandy flat that was awash with springs, and covered with trees that had never been discovered by the sawmill men. Some of them must have been a hundred feet tall. There was plenty of cover from the small plane that began coming over, now and again. We figured it was watching the dirt roads all around.

The first night we didn't even keep watch. We knew what we were doing, but they didn't, and it would take a while to get bloodhounds up from Huntsville and put them on our trail. Which, we felt sure, they wouldn't be able to follow anyway.

The middle of the second day we could hear the hounds trailing, way off in the distance. They weren't coming our way, so we didn't worry. We had a laugh at the moonshiners that were likely to be caught with their goods, with the place all full of deputies and the FBI. Our transistor radio said they had every policeman, reserve deputy, and dogcatcher in fifty miles down there in the woods looking for us. It would have been a sweet time to hit one of the bigger towns, but nobody seems to have thought of it. Anyway, we sat back and let them boil.

For the better part of a week we let things ride. According to the radio, the hunt had moved off to the north, where some poor pair of suckers had looked something like us.

But we knew how to wait things out, which is why we've done so many jobs without being caught. Then it began to rain.

Woods in fine October weather are mighty nice to live in. In chilly, wet October weather they're instant pneumonia. We needed a place to spend the next week without freezing our tails off.

All around us were big woods, never cut as far as we could see. We figured it must be some big family holding that was tied up in the courts, or some timber company would have cleaned it out. Sure enough, after looking around for a while, we found a crooked dirt track that led through thick timber to a big old tumbledown gray house.

Part of the house was empty—no windows were in the frames, the doors were black holes in the scaly walls. But the low half, behind the curving porch, was pretty tight, and smoke was coming out of the stovepipe. We scrootched under a magnolia that covered as much ground as the house did and watched for half a day.

Twice a tiny little old woman came out, once to go to the well for water, once for a trip down the brushy path to the privy. When she came back from there, she went by the woodpile and took an armload back in with her. It was getting on for dark, and we thought if she had anybody else in there, they'd have gotten the wood for her. So we went in.

She looked up when we walked in. The door hadn't been locked, though she had a portable radio going on the kitchen table, and she must've known we were or had been around close. But she didn't turn a hair. She ought to have been scared stiff, for she wasn't much taller than a ten-year-old, and wouldn't have weighed eighty pounds soaking wet. Her hair was white, and she wore it screwed up in a tight knot that pulled her eyes into a slant so you could hardly tell what color they were. They were black and bright and had a wicked light in them. I could tell when she looked up at me.

Like I say, she should have been scared. I'm six-two, and Mel is a lot bigger. We could have pinched her between our fingers, and she'd have gone out like a candle. But she just looked up at us with those slanty black eyes and said, "Good evening, gentlemen. I wondered if you weren't playing possum out in my timber stand. Come and have a cup of tea."

"Coffee," Mel grunted. "Make it strong."

"Don't buy the stuff," she said, lifting the kettle off the stove-eye. "Costs too much and gums up your innards. Mint tea or comfrey tea you can have...unless you want to go into town after coffee."

Mel stood over her and reached down. He took her by the scruff of her neck and lifted her like a cat does a kitten. He spat on the floor; then he growled at her, "Listen here, old woman, you'll do what we say, and you won't talk back. You live out here all by yourself and think maybe you count for something. You don't. We run things, when we're around, and no dried-up skirt gives us any lip. Get that, and get it good."

She looked up at him, eyes sparkling black fire, and a tight little smile twitched at her lip. Somehow, the look of that smile gave me the shivers, but I didn't mention it to Mel. He'd have hoorawed me about it. He didn't think any woman who ever lived was worth the trouble of strangling.

He thunked her down on her feet again, and she stood, hands on hips, looking at him. Up and down she surveyed him, then me. Then she said, "I'm a loner and a maverick. I thought maybe you two might be a couple more. But I was wrong. Low-life, ignorant thieves, that's all. Well, you might have had my help, but now you won't. And when Lena McCarver isn't for you, she's against you."

Mel laughed that booming laugh that didn't sound cheerful at all. Then he said, "Fix supper, woman, and shut up."

She smiled again, that tight little twitch of her lip, and moved to the cook stove to add wood. When the skillet was sizzling with bacon, Mel and I stretched out in the two fair-sized chairs in the room. The rain was chattering away on the tin roof, and it felt mighty good to be inside and warm.

When she put mugs of steamy liquid into our hands, we drank the contents, even if they did smell and taste strongly of mint. After a while, she slapped a couple of heavy plates onto the pine table and said, "Come eat. Much good may it do you." Then she started for the door at the side of the room. Mel stood up and went after her, raising his right hand to swat her across the face.

She never paused, but her right hand moved, the fingers making a funny weaving motion. Mel's hand stuck in the air, about six inches short of the spot where she had been.

"Take care, boy," she breathed. "I've been right patient with you. You raise your hand to me again, and you'll wish the FBI had you in some nice, safe prison. I'm going to my room to read, and you'll do well to dig out your manners and dust them off. Lena McCarver may not look it now, but I was reared a lady of good family, used to civility." She went through the door, leaving it open behind her.

Mel stood looking at his hand. For a half-minute it stayed stuck in mid-air; then he was able to sort of reel it in. He wiggled his fingers with a frown on his face. "Feels numb-like," he said. "Halfway between how a foot that's been asleep feels when it comes back to life, and the way it feels when you get your finger on a bare wire. What the hell did that old broad do to me?"

I pulled back a chair and sat down to pile my place with eggs and bacon and hot biscuits. "Leave her alone, Mel," I choked, between bites. "That old biddy gives me a funny feeling. She's got more on the ball, somehow, than you'd think. I feel it in my bones. Might be, we'd have done better out in the woods."

He snorted, but he sat down to eat with a thoughtful look on his ugly mug. When we were full as ticks, we opened out our bedrolls on the floor. Early as it was, we were hardly able to keep our eyes open, what with the full meal and the warm room. Before I lay down, I looked through the crack in Lena's door.

She was sitting at a little table with a coal-oil lamp in the middle. Her nose was almost touching the pages of a big, thick book, as she read, her lips moving as she moved her left index finger down the lines. Her right hand was held over the table, and she was making some sort of pattern, holding her fingers just so, crooking and wiggling them just so, until the shadow against the far wall was enough to make your skin squinch up into goose-pimples.

"What's she doing?" Mel asked, as I crept away from the door to my blankets.

"Just reading," I mumbled. But I never saw anybody read in just that way, ever before in my life. As I drifted off to sleep, the crack of light from her door seemed to grow wider and longer until it swallowed up the world...but by then, I was asleep.

The next morning was still gray and damp, and Mel was mean as a mangy hound. But I noticed he didn't snap at the old lady near as bad as he had before. Now and again he'd open his mouth with a snarly look at its corners, but she'd slant those eyes at him, and he'd just poke in more breakfast or a cigarette. Still, I could tell she was getting to him. His eyes were getting narrower and narrower and turning that dishwater gray that meant he was going to do something that might be dumb but that would surely be nasty.

About the time we were finishing eating, there came a scratch at the door, and Lena let in a piebald tomcat with ears so mauled in old fights that he barely had any at all. She put a pan of scraps on the floor behind the stove for him, and he disappeared into the corner and started giving them a fit, growling at any foot that came too near. Mel glanced over that way, then away, and I crossed my fingers. I found out the hard way about bothering old ladies' cats.

None of my preacher Pa's sermons ever taught me a thing, but old Mrs. Harrison's whaling with a stick of stove wood gave me a lot or respect for old ladies and cats.

I nudged Mel and whispered, "Let it be, Mel. It's not going to help out a bit, messing with that cat."

He just glared at me and went to the door to look out into the dismal day. By that time, the old dame was done with her dishes and had refilled the kettle and tidied up the kitchen. She looked around, nodded, then went off into the unfinished part of the house.

Mel grinned a wicked grin and eased over toward the stove. He nearly jumped out of his skin when her sharp voice said at his elbow, "'Round ten o'clock, Boze Blair will be coming out with my month's groceries. I hire him to bring me what I need, regular. If you two don't want to be seen, I'd suggest you hide in the smokehouse or the privy. If you kill Boze, his wife will have somebody out combing the woods for him, and here's where they'll look first. It's nine-ten now, so you'd better be thinking where to go."

I said, "It's mighty nasty out. Why don't we hide in the other part of the house? At least, it's got a roof."

She gave a little whinnying laugh. "Now that's a plumb good idea," she gasped. "You go right ahead and hide there. Just watch the clock, and about five to ten you go right in that door there."

I really didn't like her laugh, but I couldn't let on in front of Mel. We opened the door, and Mel sort of fooled the cat into going through. When the time came, we went in too, to find the critter sitting on a dusty mantel, looking down at us. We weren't a bit too soon, because we heard a truck coming up the drive just after.

Mel muttered through the door, "Remember, you wave him in here so we can hear every word. If anything makes him suspicious, we'll blow you both to Kingdom Come. Don't forget it."

She didn't answer, but we could see through the cracks that she was doing what he said. A scraggy old codger mooched up the steps with a big grocery box and shoved the door open with his toe. We could see glimpses of him around the door, as he set it on the table and reached for the cup of tea she handed him.

"Lots on the radio about the robbery up to Hampden," she said. "Were you there?"

"Nope," he grunted. "I come along about ten minutes too late for it. They hid out for a while, them fellers thinks, out in this direction. Minty worried some about their coming in on you, but I told her that even a bank robber wasn't going to risk the McCarver place, not to mention tackling you!" He cackled a high-pitched laugh. "Now they don't have a Chinaman's notion where them crooks is. Blocked all the roads, never thinking they might have gone ahead afoot. Fool town folks!"

Though he drank the tea and was very polite, I felt that Boze was happy to go down the steps to his truck, after Lena had paid him with crumpled bills from a leather wallet green with mildew. I turned to tell Mel that it was safe to go back in the kitchen...but he was busy.

Somehow he'd caught that tomcat and had his big hand around its neck, squeezing bit by bit. The cat's pink tongue was out between its teeth, and it was struggling mightily to free its hind feet from Mel's other hand, twisting and bucking in his fist like a fresh-caught trout.

Mel's eyes were bright and happy, and he was enjoying the critter's desperation as much as he ever enjoyed anything. I was opening my mouth to call him back to his senses when a cracked cup that had been sitting on one of the windowsills just upped and came sailing across the room and shattered against Mel's jawbone. As he stood, surprised, a glob of something black and sticky-looking oozed out of the fireplace and plopped across his wrist—the one holding the cat's hind feet.

Mel gave a yell, and his hand seemed to drop, limp, as the cat gave a heave and set to tearing Mel up with his claws. All at once, Mel had a handful of mad razorblades, and I could see little drops of his blood flying through the air every time the cat made a swipe at him. He tried to drop the cat, but now the cat had *him*, and it wasn't letting go. It climbed him as if he were a tree, leaving blood all the way; then it skittered across the mantel and made an impossible leap to the open window and out.

I went over and tried to mop Mel up with the bandana I had worn over my face in the robbery. Then I heard a giggle and turned. There stood Lena in the door, bent over, she was laughing so hard. Mel started toward her with murder in his eye, but she raised her hand and made a funny sign with her fingers.

It was like being caught in plastic...or like being a fly frozen into an ice cube that wasn't cold.

I tried my damndest to move, even if it was just to fall flat, but it was as if the air had congealed around me. My eyeballs could swivel, my lids close, but that was all of me that would move. Mel, directly in my line of vision, was in the same condition. My heart seemed to have slowed down to a leisurely ta-thump, ta-thump, and I was breathing so slowly it wasn't even noticeable.

The old woman stopped laughing and stood straight, close to Mel. If she'd been a couple of feet taller, she'd have been eyeball to eyeball with him, but as it was the top of her head came about to his second coat button. She smiled that tight smile, and her slanty eyes were bright in the gloom of the cobwebby room.

"It's been a long time since I did a really big sticky-spell," she said. "Had to study up. But it's working fine, now isn't it?"

She walked around us, and I could feel the sharpness of her eyes like thumbtacks in my back. I could hear her rummaging around in the room behind us, and cold sweat began to ooze down my back and neck. She had us cold, and there was no way of knowing what in tunket she intended to do.

Finally she came back into sight. She was carrying two big rag dolls with yarn hair and shoe-button eyes. They seemed to be clean and well kept, but their calico dresses were faded so much I knew they must be mighty old. She set the dolls on the mantel where the cat had been, propped against the mirror over it so they would sit up. Then she wiggled her fingers again, and I found my feet moving just enough so I was standing fully facing the fireplace.

She moved away—into the kitchen it seemed like, and was gone for a few seconds. Then she was back, right in front of me. She carried a footstool in one hand and a little bowl in the other. She plunked the stool down and stepped up on it, so her face was just below mine. Then she dipped her finger into the bowl, and I could see something blue on its tip, as she reached up for my forehead. I could feel the tickle as she drew a circle on my skin and several shapes or patterns inside it.

Then she got down and moved the stool, and I knew the same thing was being done to Mel. When she had finished, I could hear her pottering around putting everything away. Meanwhile, I felt as if all my insides had turned to water. I don't think I could have stood, even if she had turned me loose. Waiting for her to make her move was worse than anything she could have done...I thought.

After a bit, I heard her come back into the ruined room. She didn't come where I could see her, but I heard her muttering and sort of singing, back there by the window. It got cold, all of a sudden, as if a blue norther had hit full force. My hands and feet went completely numb; then my body began to go numb too. Even the insulated hunting jacket I wore seemed to do no goot at all.

Things went sort of dim, as if my eyes weren't working right, and the gray light in the room wavered, as if thicker clouds were going over fast. My eyes felt funnier and funnier, and then they stopped seeing at all. In the blackness, I felt as if I were moving very fast down a tunnel, but in a little the light began to come back again.

I could see the window...but from an odd angle. I could see the old woman standing there by the empty casement. I could see Mel, frozen like a statue. I could see ME! For a minute I couldn't tell what had happened. I sat there, stunned; then I tried to move my eyelids. But from the way I felt, I didn't have eyelids anymore. I slanted my gaze down as far as I could without an eyeball that moved. Two rag doll legs stuck out in front of me, with black cloth shoes on blobby feet.

Lena looked up at the mantel where I sat and grinned, a real, wide, wicked grin. Then she reached up and took me down and tucked me under one arm. As I moved, I could see that she had Mel under the other arm. She took us into the kitchen and put us where we could see the cook stove and partway down the road from the small window. We seemed to be on a high shelf, and I felt the bulk of something that seemed to be a book digging into my side. THAT book, I thought, with a shudder.

"I don't want to be too mean to you boys," Lena cackled.

"Don't want you to be too bored and unhappy. This way, you can see what goes on—what there is of it—and maybe you'll do some thinking. I'm going to get enough work out of you to pay for all my trouble."

I could hear her tiny feet pattering back through the door, then returning—followed by the clunk, clunk of heavy feet in thick boots. They moved across the kitchen and out onto the porch, tap-tap-tap; CLUNK, CLUNK, CLUNK!

Through the window, I watched them move down the road toward the woods. I carried a crosscut saw over my shoulder, and Mel had two axes in one hand and wedges in the other. A bottle of oil stuck out of his hip pocket.

She went in front. One hand was in the air above her shoulder, beating time. Our feet, following obediently, kept to her beat.

We sit on the shelf, Mel and I. Sometimes she moves us around. Sometimes she plays with us as if she were still ten years old.

Mostly we sit. And think.

The young tend to think we old people are weak and helpless. Well, we may not be a strong as once we were, but what we lose in strength we gain in meanness.

THAT OLD BIDDY

Denny and me was a team, you know? We got away with murder in school, stealin' other kids' lunch money, shopliftin' from downtown stores, muggin' old women. By the time we got expelled, we was shaking down old folks for their Social Security checks. When one of 'em killed himself on account of not having eatin' money, things got hot for us. We decided to take a hike until it was safe to come back to the city.

Denny had a grandpa lived out in the boonies, and we hitched a ride part way, then stole a car and drove up in style. The shanty was nothin' much, and the grandpa was on his last legs, not able to run us off. The little chicken-run town was too small for much, but we kept our hands in by sneakin' into houses at night and stealin' what we could.

Made quite a stir, I tell you. They hadn't had a robbery in so long that nobody ever locked a door at night. The only law was a constable that lived twenty miles away, and that poor fool couldn't find his own tail with both hands and a road map.

Denny and me had a high-heeled old time, you better believe. Got so the folks even started lockin' their cars, which they'd never done in their lives unless they visited the city. We had all them little old widows scared out of their drawers.

We'd dumped the stolen car in the river. No way we'd be dumb enough to drive it, when there had to be notices out on the license number. No, we just "borrowed" cars at night, because a lot of folks still couldn't remember to lock 'em up. We'd drive into Linton, go to a picture show, buy what we needed at the all-night grocery store, and mail the extra bucks to my Uncle Ned, who would hold the money for us till we could risk going back.

Things went along, sweet and smooth, for the better part of a year. At least, they went fine as far as business was concerned. We just about died of boredom. There was no—I mean NO—action. No girls, no booze (the place was dry and intended to stay that way), not even a poker game. We got so desperate we even went fishin', for god's sake!

We kept asking Grandpa about the local folks, of course, but he was so ga-ga he didn't remember things except by fits and starts. It took us ten months to find out about Miz Biddy Livingstone.

We'd seen the overgrown driveway that went to her house, of course, but it wasn't any different from the ones going to chicken farms or hay meadows. Who'd have thought there was a big house behind all those trees, and inside lived the only really rich human being around Cricket Hollow?

Understand, we didn't rush into anything. We might be young, but we wasn't fools. We found out everything we could from the old man, which wasn't much. Then we sneaked through the woods and watched that house, takin' our time, figurin' out what she did every day and when.

The way she lived, you'd think she was dirt poor. At sunrise she was out feeding her chickens and the old mule that lived in a patch behind her house. She had no more use for that mule than we did, but she fed it as if it still pulled a plow. About nine or so she'd come out of the house again and work in her vegetable garden. Then she'd check her fences or cut wood in her wood-lot or some such, though according to grandpa she could've hired everything done or moved to town and lived without workin' at all. Crazy old biddy!

She wasn't very big, though she was sort of square-built, like she'd been fairly strong in her day. Her hair had gone so thin we could see the sun shining off her scalp when she went outside without her big straw hat. She was about five-foot nothin', and everybody knows old women are pretty weak, with brittle bones. We figured that if we went about it smart and sneaky, we could get into her house and find her stash of cash without her ever knowin' it until too late.

Still, we hadn't got where we were by being careless. We acted normal as anything, going to town for the old man in daytime, pretendin' we'd come to take care of him since he got so feeble. Folks got used to us and even seemed to think a lot of us for doin' that. We even got introduced to Constable Stark, when he come to town for a church supper.

We never asked another soul about Miz Livingstone, and Grandpa couldn't recall anything from one day to the next. Far as anybody knew, we didn't know she existed. That was just what we wanted.

Things rocked along till winter, which in our part of the country comes about the first of November and is more wet than cold. We'd set around the fireplace, with Grandpa on his cot close enough to keep him warm, and swap tales or jokes or plans for the future.

One night we forgot ourselves just a little and tried some of the homemade wine we'd made that summer out of wild plums and sugar and yeast. It was stronger than you'd think, and we all three got a little high.

Denny and I started talkin', in a general way, about robberies. Grandpa chirked up more than he had in months and began talkin' a blue streak.

"You mention stealin', boys. I tried that once, when I was young and ignorant. Got in with the Youngblood boys from across the river, and they was mean and ornery as folks can get. They decided to rob old Miz Livingstone's folks, the Fosters, up at the big house in the woods.

"Everybody knew they had money, and Sal and Rooster talked me into goin' to that house with 'em one night. At the last minute, I got so scared I mighty nigh puked, and they laughed at me and went ahead, leavin' me out in the yard, sick as a poisoned dog."

Denny opened his mouth to ask a question, but I stopped him. Grandpa never got back to the same place you stopped him at, and we'd be sure to miss the end of this story and get the start of some other we didn't care about. Sure enough, he plowed right ahead, which he wouldn't have done if he'd been asked anything.

"I got rid of everything I had, down to my shoe laces, but by then I was out of the notion of taking up robbery. So I waited. And I waited. I waited till sunrise, and no Sal and no Rooster ever come back, though old Mr. Foster went out to milk their cow right on time."

I wanted to ask a question now, but I knew better. Holdin' my breath, I waited to see if Grandpa would keep on talkin'.

He sighed long and gusty, cleared his throat, and looked into the fire. "Nobody never seen Sal and Rooster Youngblood again. I taken it that they got the money and skedaddled without stoppin' to speak to me. Wouldn't have blamed 'em for that. But their folks never heard a word either, and it's been—lordy, it's been sixty-five year or more since that day."

Well, Denny and I nodded at each other. We'd left home too, and nobody but my Uncle Ned, who had been in stir and knew the ropes, would ever hear from us again either. Still, it was funny that the Fosters never made any stink about being robbed.

"Ever been any talk about where they kept their cash?" Denny asked, keeping his tone casual.

The old man cackled. "Been lots of speculatin' but no provin'," he said. "I think they kept it where anybody who lived through the Big Depression keeps any cash he might have. Under the mattress. Only safe place there is."

Well, it was sure and certain that if Grandpa happened to have any money that was where it might be, but we sort of steered clear of robbin' him yet. He was Denny's grandpa, after all. But it sounded reasonable that if the Youngbloods didn't get all the cash and ran off out of fear, the old woman might just hide it under her mattress. Old folks seem to be alike, when it comes down to it.

We climbed trees around that old house, peepin' in windows after dark to see which one was hers. The downstairs was only three rooms, one great big kitchen on one side of the entrance hall, and two fairly big ones on the other. Parlor and dining room, I guessed.

Upstairs there was only one room ever lit after dark, and that had to be old Biddy's bedroom.

* * * * * * *

We decided to take advantage of her work in the garden, which even in November was still goin' as she banked rows of collard greens or laid down compost on the rest. We climbed the big ash tree that rose beside a front window and managed to get the thing open without breakin' it. Wasn't even locked, if you can believe that!

We had hoped to search her bedroom while she was out, so we headed down the long, dingy hall toward the back. Before we could get there we heard the back door creak open and slam shut, and slow steps start up the stairs. What a disappointment! We'd just have to come back at night. If she woke up—well, it would be weeks before anybody checked on her, and by that time we'd be gone, with nothing to connect us to her death. Includin' Grandpa.

We'd made up our minds, so it was time to get the thing done. If she was as rich as we thought, we'd be able to drive Grandpa's old pickup to Houston, abandon it in some junk yard, then fly anyplace we decided to go. The plan was foolproof.

That night it was chilly and damp, though not actually rainin'. We slunk through the woods on foot, not wantin' anybody on the road to remember seeing the old pickup out of its place. Dead leaves flapped and the ground squished under our feet; a mournful owl hooted among the trees.

I was so excited that nothing bothered me, and warm, almost boundin' along, with Denny trampin' silently behind me. When we got within sight of the house, the upstairs light was already on. She worked hard and went to bed early. We crept up on the wide veranda to get out of the damp. The light from her window made a bright square against the shrubbery around at the side of the house, and we could keep an eye on it from the end of our shelter.

It went out before we were quite ready, but that was all right. We wanted to give her plenty of time to get to sleep. It would be better for everybody if she slept right through being robbed.

When the house had been dark for a couple of hours, we climbed that tree again and checked out the window. It was still unlocked, and now it was easy to open, for we had unstuck it before.

Slippin' inside, we crossed the floor in our sock feet and eased the door open without any noise.

The door to Biddy's room was closed but, of course, not locked. It swung open on oiled hinges. I went down on all-fours, and Denny did the same. We crawled forward, guidin' ourselves by the dark shapes of furniture against the pale sky beyond the windows.

The old woman sighed and turned on the bed, and that gave us the right direction. Denny slid up one side and I went up the other, and we started working our hands up under the mattress. It was thick and heavy and smelled stale and old, like the woman on top of it.

She turned again, almost mashin' my arm flat, and I was still as a ghost. I listened for Denny but couldn't hear a thing. Then something touched the top of my head—something cold and hard and round. It tapped twice, and I caught my breath. Another tap, harder this time. I nodded against the pressure.

Then I heard Denny gasp and I wondered how she managed to be on both sides of the bed at once. For an instant the pressure disappeared. Then I heard a thump, followed by a groan, and I figured that Denny had knocked her out. I rose to my feet and found a rifle barrel against my mouth.

It pushed me back, there was a click, and the bedside lamp came on, to show me a dumpy little old woman in a long nightgown, holding the rifle as steady as death itself. Beyond the bed I could see Denny's back. He wasn't movin'.

"Lady....," I began, but she cut me off.

"Shut up, boy. I know what you're here for and you're not the first to come here for the same thing. My daddy killed a couple of young thieves when I was a girl. Buried them in the new-tilled garden ground. Nobody ever looked for 'em here, and if they had they wouldn't have found 'em.

"I've had to take care of a few more in my time. Good rich garden ground I have out there. You'll fit right in. Now pick up your friend there. No use an old woman like me having to strain her back toting two husky boys so far.

"Move!"

So there I was with Denny over my shoulder, edgin' down those steep stairs. My shadow looked like a monster ahead of me, and behind me was that awful old woman, who had swapped her rifle for a big revolver that ought to be too heavy for her even to lift.

We went through the kitchen, out of the back door, down the path toward the garden, invisible in the misting rain. Denny groaned and almost waked up, but there was another thump and he went limp again. He was the lucky one.

"Stop here," she said. "Put him down right there. Kick that mulch back—yes, like that. Good. Likely you never did anything that useful before in your life."

Shakin', sobbin' under my breath, I did what she said, knowing there was no use beggin'.

Those dark eyes had never shown mercy in her life, I felt sure. Her face was calm, her mouth a straight line as she nodded again.

The pistol rose in her pudgy hand. The hammer went back. I screamed and passed out.

When I came to, I was here in the constable's office, and Denny was lying where he now sits.

She'd done the whole thing to punish us, to scare us, and lord knows she did what she intended.

Thank God we hadn't killed Grandpa yet! And we didn't get a chance to kill Biddy Livingstone, which may or may not be a good thing.

I'm still shakin', and I'm still scared, because they've got a deputy on his way from the city with a murder warrant. That old bastard who killed himself left a note, damn him! We'll be charged with murder, the constable tells me, even if we didn't snuff anybody local.

So here we are, lookin' at life—or worse—and Uncle Ned'll spend every dime I sent him for the last year.

It just ain't fair!

ACKNOWLEDGMENTS

"You Can't Go Home Again" was first published in *The Horror Show*, Winter, 1988.

"Down in the Bottomlands" was first published in *East Texas Outdoorsman*, February 1988.

"Lonesome Canefield Blues" was first published in *New Mystery*, Vol. 1, Issue 1.

"Hallimore's Dog" was first published in *Dead of Night*, Spring, 1995.

"Fungus Grows in the Dark" was first published in *Hardboiled*, 1994.

"Stalking Woman" was first published in *New Frontiers* anthology, 1990.

"A Most Genteel Pursuit" was first published in *Alfred Hitchcock's Mystery Magazine*, February, 1995.

"The Creek, It Done Riz" was first published in *Cold Blood*, edited by Richard T. Chizmar, Mark V. Ziesing, 1991.

"Coon Hunt with Distractions" was first published by *Weirdbook*, Autumn, 1990.

"Crawfish" was first published in *Psychological Perspectives* in 1971, and in *Alfred Hitchcock's Stories to Be Read with the Lights On*, 1973.

"The Wallow" was first published in *Noir*, 1994.

"Stiff Sentence" was first published in *Hardboiled*, 1994.

"Digging Up Arthur" was first published in *Mystery Scene Reader*, 1987.

"Night of the Cougar" was first published in *Best of the West*, edited by Joe R. Lansdale, Doubleday, 1986.

ABOUT THE AUTHOR

The author of sixty-two books, more than forty of them published commercially, **ARDATH MAYHAR** began her career in the early eighties with science fiction novels from Doubleday and TSR. Atheneum published several of her young adult and children's novels. Changing focus, she wrote westerns (as **Frank Cannon**) and mountain man novels (as **John Killdeer**), four prehistoric Indian books under her own name, and historical western *High Mountain Winter* under the byline **Frances Hurst**.

Recently she has been working with on-line publishers. *A Road of Stars* was her first original novel to appear in print-on-demand format. Many of her out-of-print titles are now available from e-publishers fictionwise.com and renebooks.com; many other novels are being published by the Borgo Press Imprint of Wildside Press and Amazon.com.

Now in her seventies, Mayhar was widowed in 1999, after forty-one years of marriage, and has four grown sons. She now works at home, writing short fiction and nonfiction, and doing book doctoring professionally. Her web pages can be found at:

w2.netdot.com/ardathm/ and
http://ofearna.us/ books/mayhar.html

www.ingramcontent.com/pod-product-compliance
Lightning Source LLC
Chambersburg PA
CBHW051919240626
47153CB00004B/1281

*9 7 8 1 4 3 4 4 0 3 5 2 0 *